Blurb

Wow, there she stood, Vena Thorn, the one that got away. Tyler Kinson never thought that he would ever lay eyes on her again. This vision was older but more beautiful and angelic then she was eight years ago. Oh, how he regretted letting her walk out of his life, but never again. She was captured and branded but didn't have a clue. Yet.

After being brutalized by her " Ex," Vena had no intentions of ever loving another man and that included her best friend, Tyler Kinson. As much as she missed their friendship, she held tormented secrets close to her heart. Ones that Tyler could never know. But Tyler's hot pursuit could convince her to give love another try. So, ignoring her fears, she allowed herself one magical night in his arms. Would her fears hold true? Would he stay? or would he walk away?

Dedication

Lena H.
My Collaborator
My Sister, My Friend, My Muse

Acknowledgements
Lee Summers
Editor

Cover Design
Renee Luke
Cover Me – Book Covers

Chapter One

"Look at that crowd, Tyler," Samuel Carson replied excitedly to his boss as they looked at the monitor in the security office of the restaurant.

"Yeah, this is the biggest crowd yet. Looks like they're wrapped around the building," Tyler replied, smiling as the cameras scanned the crowd.

Samuel looked over at his boss with pride. He had been with Tyler Kinson when he opened his first Den restaurant some fifteen years ago. Tyler knew all there was to know about the food and beverage industry. He kept on top of any changes in the field, making him one of the most knowledgeable and popular restaurateurs in the Midwest. He was the founder and owner of the ever-trendy Den Restaurants Franchise. After many years of hard work and dedication, he was finally satisfied with his accomplishments. He had opened his Illinois restaurants in Chicago, Springfield, Naperville, and most recently, Rockford. Sam was never prouder of his boss and friend. Samuel turned his attention to the line of people dressed in their finery, waiting to experience the first-class service and ambiance of one of the most popular restaurants in the Midwest.

The Den's superb cuisine, atmosphere, and service were their trademark. Every person commissioned to work for 'The Den' was trained to Tyler's specifications. His employees qualified in basic restaurant skills such as table setting and the correct way to pour wine, going as far as mastering the proper way to greet the guests. The highly paid formal servers were assigned only five tables in the dining room where they were to assure that each guest received first-class service from the time they entered the dining room until they left. Tyler was adamant about the well-being and comfort of his guests, and if the server could not handle that, they were fired on the spot.

The difference in this Den and others was that it was larger and offered additional services. This Den provided banquet rooms, conference rooms on the upper floors, catering to professional businesspersons, and any social events a client desired. After six months of extensive research in Rockford, Illinois, Tyler was pleased with what he discovered. The large vacant building, which had formerly been a three-story department store, was perfect for his greatest and most significant restaurant. As luck would have it, Tyler also discovered the small suburban town called Northbrook just a few miles outside of Rockford, and there is where he commissioned to have his dream house built. It was time to get out of Chicago. Lately, life had become mundane and, he hated to admit, lonely. He also needed a change and was ready to settle down. He had worked hard for twenty years to get here. He now felt the need to slow down and enjoy what he had accomplished, wanting and needing that peace and serenity he so rightly deserved.

"I think we're going to be successful, Sam," Tyler absently replied as he gazed at the monitor.

"Did you doubt it?" Sam replied, smiling.

"I don't know. I did have some misgivings, but looks as if everything is running smoothly, I'm pleased to say."

He was now fifty-two years old, divorced, childless, and wealthy. Often he wondered whether this was the life he had chosen. It was fortunate he had no children; his ex-wife didn't want them. She was too vain and selfish to share her spotlight with a kid. Janice was her happiest when she was spending his money or parading around town with her uppity group of friends that he could not stand. They constantly and tirelessly argued over the same thing day in and day out, so the marriage ended. Of course, her alimony was more than she deserved, but he paid it just to be rid of her. Overall, he was very pleased with his accomplishments, even if occasional loneliness reared its ugly head. He learned to cope, but still there was something missing in his life, an emptiness he couldn't explain. The thought of getting married again was out of the question. He didn't want another Janice. However, he did have his share of casual relationships, as long as the women knew that's all it was - casual. Now, even those were getting tiresome.

Times like this made him remember his grandmother. If only she had lived to see all his successes. He was born and raised on Chicago's south side, where the streets were tough and living was hard. However, he had a tougher and harder grandmother, who raised him when his mother overdosed on heroin when he was seven. Never knew his father; with the lifestyle his mother led, it could have been anyone. Although his grandmother, whom he called Mama, was hard-hitting and strict, there was love and lots of it. She had vowed she was not going to let him fall by the wayside like his mother, in a city that would suck you in if you allowed it. Every day she would tell him, *"There's a good life out there for you. Come hell or high water, I'm gonna see that you get it."* And he did get it. Mama worked hard to see him through Kendall College. He received his MA degree in Culinary, Food, Hotel, and Restaurant Management, graduating at the top of his class. He was offered a top salaried job, and Mama was immensely proud of him.

When the money started rolling in, right away he and Mama moved out of Chicago and into the suburban town of McKinley Park. With a lot of prodding, he was able to convince Mama to stop working and enjoy her remaining years. He was glad she lived to see him open his first *Den*, and he has never known a prouder moment than at that opening, for he knew his Mama loved him with all her heart.

Tyler stopped his preoccupation with the past and focused on the monitors. The trial opening was an enormous success, and he was happy. It would be a few more months before the official grand opening, which was after the completion of the entire building.

Tyler turned his attention back to the line of people outside the restaurant as the camera's continued to scan the crowd.

Tyler froze; his eyes widened when he saw a familiar face from his past. Her maple coloring and perfect oval face was as flawless as he remembered. Those temptingly curved full lips he'd always wanted to taste and that cute delicate, dainty nose were still the same. He could see she still wore her dark brown hair pulled tightly back. He would never forget that face as long as he lived.

"Stop scanning," he exclaimed to the security technician.

"Scan back; yes, right there. Zoom in on her," he ordered.

A smile came to his handsome face. "Vena Thorn," he said, sounding almost breathless. Samuel looked at Tyler and frowned.

"You know her?" he asked.

"Yes, I know her," he answered, his eyes on the screen.

"Sam, I want you to go into that crowd and get her and whoever is with her. Bring them in and take them to the Solarium. I'll radio down and have a table set with VIP service. Have a bottle of our best champagne chilling before they get there. I want our best waiter and service for the ladies; anything they want," Tyler ordered, trying not to sound too anxious. Sam looked at him strangely. He hadn't seen Tyler this excited in years. Tyler looked at Sam, grinning broadly.

"Classy," he whispered.

"So what do I tell this Vena for the reason she is being brought inside?" Sam asked.

"Tell her an old friend wants her party to join their table."

"Okay, Ty, I'm on it," Sam assured him before leaving.

****

Vena, Hanna, Dee, and Mary stood in the overcrowded line. Vena looked behind her, and an uneasy feeling settled over her. She loved these three women, but she didn't like being around all these people. Why did she let them talk her into coming to this opening? Hanna looked over at her.

"Come on Vee, you look petrified," Hanna said taking her hand.

"Hanna, why did you bring me here? It's too many people. You know I don't like being in crowds," she stated, wringing her hands.

"It's okay Vee," Dee said, taking her hands in her own. "You need this, honey. It's time to start living again."

"Why didn't we just go to a movie then?" she asked, looking from one face to the other.

"Because, Vee," Mary replied, "that is not getting out."

Mary's brown eyes scanned the crowd. "This is exciting. When I heard about the newest Den opening so close to Northbrook, I thought this would be the perfect celebration for you after five years of hiding in that loft."

"I was not hiding," Vena replied indignantly.

"You were hiding," the three women stated in unison. Vena rolled her eyes and looked away.

"You looked pretty, honey," Hanna stated smiling.

Vena glared at her friends with a smile hovering on her lips. "You three are so lucky I love you."

These four ladies all met when Vena first moved to Northbrook ten years ago and became fast friends.

They all grinned at her, causing Vena to smile. She silently watched as these wonderful ladies laughed and talked. Hanna Jackson was forty-six, with skin the color of rich mahogany and short, curly hair that complimented her round face. She was a buyer for a large department store, divorced, and had no children. She was of medium height, with a voluptuous curvy figure. Hanna was outspoken, energetic, funny, and confident. Vena smiled; she didn't know what she would do without Hanna in her life.

Vena's eyes moved to Mary Willows and she smiled fondly. Mary was her married friend and extremely devoted to her husband Tom and two children. She was forty-five years old with impeccable tawny skin and medium length auburn hair that framed her small oval face. A registered head nurse at Glenview Hospital, Mary was soft spoken, motherly and kind. Then there was Dee Caldwell, the youngest of the group. At forty years old, although she looked to be thirty-something at the most, Dee was an uncommonly striking woman and attracted her share of attention from the opposite sex. She had that statuesque supermodel's body, a lovely wild honey coloring with sandy blonde hair, and a sprinkle of freckles on her dainty nose, which men found incredibly sexy, or so they said. Dee owned a popular and successful beauty salon in downtown Northbrook. She was single and preferred it that way. Like Hanna, she dated many and often. Dee was shy in some ways, bold in others and loved a good time. These three women were the sisters of her heart, and if anyone wanted to know, these three women had saved her from herself a few years ago. They had formed a bond which no one could break. They saw Vena through the worst times in her life and were still immensely supportive and protective.

Vena's eyes scanned the area and noticed an exceptionally attractive middle-aged man making his way through the throng of people waiting for a table in the renowned Den restaurant. He stopped briefly and appeared to be searching for someone. She also noticed that he had one of those earpieces in his ear and stopped walking for a second to listen to whoever was talking on the other end. He moved toward them and stopped. Vena stepped away from him, reaching for

Hanna's hand. Hanna looked over at Vena, concerned when she noticed the handsome man standing in front of her.

"Hello, handsome, can we help you?" Hanna said, smiling saucily.

"Yes, you can," Sam replied, smiling at the sexy woman with the full lips.

"Sam!" Tyler said through the earpiece.

"Right, right," Sam muttered, grinning." Ms. Vena Thorn, I am Samuel Carson, General Manager of The Den. I have been told that an old friend awaits the pleasure of you and your party's company at his table," Sam stated smiling.

Vena's hand tightened on Hanna's hand.

"I don't have an old friend," Vena whispered nervously to Hanna.

"Who is this old friend?" Hanna asked as Dee and Mary moved closer to them.

"Please, ladies, follow me, and you shall see," Sam invited with a broad smile on his face.

The girls looked at Vena. "Hey," Dee said, "let's see who this old friend is."

"We don't know this man maybe…" Vena countered, chewing nervously on her lower lip.

"Vee, it's alright. Plus, we get out of this long ass line," Hanna stated. "And if we don't know him, we will kick him in his little ballies and leave." Dee and Mary laughed.

Vena remained silent, gnawing on her bottom lip. "Okay, but…"

"Well, Sam, lead on," Hanna said flirtatiously.

"Good," Sam said, smiling at Hanna. "Follow me, ladies."

Tyler smiled at Sam's antics. He shook his head and watched as the ladies followed Sam out of line. He felt an excitement in the hollow of his stomach. His Vena. She was older but still as beautiful as he remembered. Years ago, she had left his employ to follow her dream of opening a dance studio, and he often wondered over the years how she was doing. Since that day she walked out of his life, he had somehow lost all contact with her. He always thought he and Vena would be business partners someday. His thoughts filtered back to when she had resigned from his employ, as if it happened just yesterday. Tyler was angry and felt his best friend had deserted him. He selfishly assumed she would follow him in his dreams and goals. However, it was only after she left that he realized he had never once asked her if she had any dreams or goals of her own, and he since regretted that he never had. She had believed in him. Not once did she doubt he would succeed, and she encouraged him not to give up when things seemed to not happen as fast as he had craved. The day she presented her resignation to him, he was livid. He knew dancing was her passion, but not so much that she would give up her well-paying job for something that was not a reliable career, he questioned it. Suffice it to say, he did not handle the news of Vena's leaving well. He said things that he knew hurt her, and in her way, she quietly told him to go to hell. That was the last time he had seen or heard from her. A few days later, he tried to call her apartment, but her phone was no longer in service - nor her cell. He had gone to her apartment, only to be informed by her landlord that she had moved. That was that. His best friend had left him because of his selfishness.

Tyler recalled the first time he'd met Vena Thorn. He hired her as his restaurant manager at the Grand Hotel in Chicago where he was General Manager. The first thing he thought during the interview was that she was the most beautiful woman he had ever encountered, and she was dressed to impress. He was indeed impressed. She was recently widowed with two young children, and she didn't mind voicing that she needed a job. Her education and resume were impressive, and her classy, sophisticated appearance was just an added bonus.

As the years passed, they worked very closely together and really got to know one another. Therefore, Tyler ensured that he maintained nothing more than a friendly relationship with Vena. Surprisingly, he found he enjoyed their friendship, and that meant more to him than anything. He knew anything more between them would destroy the friendship they shared. Vena was intelligent and elegant, with a great sense of humor, but was still a little naïve when it came to some of life's situations. When she hooked up with John Matthews, he had to admit he was a bit jealous. He instantly knew John was no good for her. He recalled the many times she had cried on his shoulder about John and his treatment of her, and many times he had advised her to leave him. She just say she loved John in her own way, but Tyler knew she stayed with him out of pity. He knew for a fact John Matthews had used her kindness and compassion for him every time she threatened to leave him. Every time she took him back, she would say to Tyler, *"He has no family, and everybody needs somebody."* All he knew was John was a lucky man and didn't know it or deserve her. He hoped that she was finally rid of him. Tyler took a deep breath and left the security office to meet his Classy. He couldn't believe it; he had the nerve to have butterflies in his stomach.

****

Sam led the girls to a beautiful glass-enclosed room. Vanilla scented candlelight glowed throughout the dimly lit room, giving it that romantic aura. A few small round tables intricately set were beautifully exhibited around the room.

"Oh my, this is beautiful," Mary said breathlessly, looking around.

"It's so romantic," Dee gushed.

"Yeah," Vena agreed, "but I don't have any old friend."

Sam smiled. A young man stood beside him. "James will be your butler for this evening, and your old friend will join you shortly," Sam said before he turned to leave the room.

"Oh, Sam," Hanna called seductively. She went to him and handed him her card. "Call me."

The girls shook their heads and chuckled. James seated each lady, ensuring her comfort. He filled the ladies' glasses with champagne and returned the bottle to the ice bucket that sat beside the table. Vena looked utterly confused, and Hanna, Dee, and Mary looked astonished.

"Who is this person who knows you, Vee?" Mary inquired before taking a sip of her champagne.

"This is the best champagne I have ever tasted," Dee stated as she took another sip from her glass.

"Taste it, Vee," Hanna encouraged.

Vena lifted the glass to her lips and sipped it. The girls watched closely. Vena smiled.

"Hey, she likes it," Hanna said, laughing.

James returned and stood by the table. "Ladies, how may I serve you?" James asked formally, extending each lady a large leather-bound menu. Each woman looked at him. James smiled. "You may have anything your heart desires."

"Ms. Thorn, I understand that you have a fondness for lump crabmeat sautéed in garlic with drawn butter?"

Vena frowned at the man. "Yes, how did you know that?" Vena asked suspiciously.

James smiled. "Shall I serve it?" Vena just looked at him.

"We will all have the crabmeat," Hanna stated.

James moved around the table refilling glasses before leaving them alone.

"Vee, you have no idea who this could be?" Dee asked curiously.

Vena shook her head. "The only old friend I have that would know my weakness for lump crab is Tyler Kinson."

"Tyler Kinson?"

"Yes, I knew him a long time ago. I haven't seen him in about ten years though."

"Oh, that's your boss from Chicago, right?" Mary asked, remembering that Vee mentioned him a time or two.

Vena nodded. "Yes, I worked as his restaurant manager before I moved to Northbrook," she replied.

"Yes, I remember you briefly talking about it," Dee replied. "Well, do you think it's him?"

Vena shrugged. "I don't know; we lost touch a long time ago."

"Well, whoever it is, I want to thank him personally for this delicious champagne," Hanna stated, grinning and lifting the glass to her lips.

Another server came and poured more champagne in the girls' glasses. Even Vena was on her third glass, which was going straight to her head. She was not a drinker, but the champagne was positively delicious.

James returned with the dishes of crabmeat and placed a plate in front of each woman.

"Have you decided what you want for the main course, ladies?" he asked.

"We haven't even looked," they each admitted, giggling.

"Well, would you mind if I chose for you?" he asked cordially.

"No, please James. I'm sure everything is wonderful," Hanna replied with a coy smile.

"Splendid," he bowed before leaving.

The girls dug into the crabmeat with gusto while the server popped the cork on another bottle of champagne and again refilled their glasses. The girls were now giggling and talking animatedly. Even Vena began to relax and enjoy herself.

"Hello, Classy," a familiar deep voice said in the room.

Vena's head snapped around, and she looked over her shoulder when she heard that familiar baritone voice. She stood and stared, stunned. Her jaw dropped open in surprise.

Tyler moved towards her as Vena pushed the chair way from the table.

Vena," he said softly. She was as dainty as he remembered.

"Tyler," she cried breathlessly.

Tyler's arms opened, and Vena wasted no time running to him.

Her arms wrapped around his neck, and he lifted her from the floor, holding her tight.

"I've missed you so much," she whispered in his ear.

"You still my girl?" he countered softly.

"Always," she whispered.

Oblivious to the people around them, they continued to hold on to each other. Mary, Dee, and Hanna exchanged brief glances at each other before openly staring at the embracing couple. Vena was always so refined and reserved that it stunned them to see her openly displaying affection in public.

"Tyler," she said with bated breath and kissed him on his lips.

For just a second, Tyler was dumbfounded, especially when her tongue caressed his lower lip and raised his pulse ten times its normal rate. Vena had never kissed him other than in a brotherly manner, and this kiss was far from that. Tyler was the first to break the kiss and placed her on her feet, looking at her with questioning eyes.

"I don't believe you are here, Tyler," she replied, still astonished. Tyler smiled and led her back to her friends.

Tyler held Vena's chair as she sat, and he took a seat beside her.

Vena could not take her eyes off his handsome face. Tyler Kinson, her best friend, was sitting beside her. If this was a dream, she never wanted to wake up.

Hanna spoke first, frowning at Vena. She believes the girl has totally forgotten they are with her. "Hi, I'm Hanna; this is Dee and Mary."

"Hi," the girls said in unison.

"Hello, I'm Tyler Kinson. It's great to meet you."

Vena was so busy looking at Tyler, she missed the introductions. Her eyes never left his face.

"Vena?" Hanna called loudly, frowning at her friend. She was always getting on them about decorum, and here she was doing something that was so out of character, the girls were in shock at her behavior.

"No more of this wonderful champagne for Vena," Mary said, chuckling as Hanna and Dee laughed in agreement.

"What?" she frowned sheepishly. "It's been a long time since I've seen him; ten years, huh?" Vena said, turning her attention back to Tyler.

Tyler felt her small hand take his hand under the table. "Are you drunk, Vena?" Tyler asked with a smile.

Looking quite shocked, "I don't get drunk," she announced incredulously. "I'm..."

"Slightly inebriated," the group finished for her, including Tyler, causing them all to laugh together.

"You do know her well," Hanna smiled at Tyler. He nodded and smiled back.

"Why haven't you ever told us about Tyler, Vena?" Dee asked.

"I thought I did. We knew each other in Chicago. We worked together for many years, he taught me the restaurant business, and we became friends. There was really nothing to tell."

"What brings you to Rockford?" Mary asked.

"I'm opening another restaurant here in Rockford, but I'm living in Northbrook now," he responded.

"Northbrook? That's where we live," Vena stared, astonished. "Are you still managing?" she asked.

"Yeah, for myself; I own The Den Enterprises," he said proudly.

"What?" the girls exclaimed.

"Those are fabulous places. I went to the one in Chicago with some clients. Very impressive," Hanna said with enthusiasm. "Remember, I told you guys about that?"

"Some of my co-workers said the place was great," Mary added. "How many are there now?"

"This is my fifth and last," he answered.

Vena smiled at him. "So, you followed your dream; that's great. I'm proud of you," she said and then kissed him on his cheek. "I always knew you would do it."

"Thank you, Classy. That means a lot coming from you." He smiled at her and found himself getting mesmerized by her lovely face. *This is still my girl,* he thought with pride. Classy was the nickname he had given her many years ago, and she was still as classy as he remembered.

"Another round, ladies?" Tyler asked and signaled the server.

"Did you open your studio?" he inquired.

"Yes, I did. It's great. I'm now looking into starting my own dance company, but it's coming terribly slow. However, the studio does well.

She tilted her head to look at him. "I can't believe you remember that."

"Why wouldn't I? Classy, it was your dream; your dreams meant a lot to me."

"Come on, Tyler, that's not what you said ten years ago," she said reprovingly.

"Well, let me take this time to ask your forgiveness for being selfish. I didn't want you to leave me. I always thought we would build together."

Vena smiled. "I forgive you," she said, as warm glow flowed through her.

Hanna, Mary, and Dee watched as Vena and Tyler talked as if they were not there; the two looked at one another with smiles. The girls watched them and thought there had to be something between Tyler and Vena other than friendship.

Hanna, being the most audacious of the four women, looked from Tyler to Vena and stated unambiguously, "You two had a fling ten years ago."

"No, no, we are just friends; strictly friends," they both stated.

"Yeah, and you expect me to believe that you two have never…" Hanna said.

"Never," Vena said. "Tyler's married."

"Was married," he interjected.

"I'm sorry it didn't work out," she said earnestly.

Tyler shrugged. "It wasn't supposed to, Classy. You knew how Janice was."

Vena nodded as she sipped her drink.

"Hey," Hanna said with a puckered brow, looking at the two of them. "You two had to have an affair."

"Hanna," Vena said indignantly, "I don't do that."

"No, I wanted to, but she doesn't do that," Tyler joked.

Vena gasped with surprise. "That's not funny, Tyler," Vena said and chuckled in spite of herself.

Vena was in heaven. Tyler was beside her and looking just as good as she remembered. Perhaps a little older, but he looked good with his straight patrician nose with the slightly flaring nostrils, his defined jaw line, and his bow-shaped full mouth. He still had a full head of dark hair, cut close and gracefully graying at the temples. She had missed him very much these past years, and he was never far from her thoughts. She listened as he talked to her friends, savoring the rich baritone of his voice. She smiled. Still the same charming Tyler she remembered.

Vena noted that the girls seemed to like Tyler, and when it came to her, they were like mother hens. She knew they did not ever want her to get hurt as she did with John. John was a monster. He had done his worst to her, and it took her a long time to come back. After John, Vena vowed no more relationships; she did not want to take the chance of getting hurt like that ever again. She told them, "At fifty years old, what do I need with a relationship?"

They all talked, feasted on an excellent dinner and laughed easily, enjoying each other's company. Vena couldn't remember being this relaxed in a long time. It felt right.

Finishing the final round of drinks, it was obvious to all at the table that Vena was a little more than tipsy, although she tried hard to conceal it and was handling herself well.

"Well, everyone," Mary said, "I must get home to my man. Tyler, it was nice meeting you, and we hope to see you again soon," she said with deep meaning. "Come, girls, I'm driving."

Tyler stood up. He hated to see Vena go. Tyler shook each of the girls' hand.

"Great seeing you, Ty," Vena said. "Call me." She left them and walked slowly toward the door.

Unknown to Vena, Hanna motioned for Tyler to take Vena home.

Tyler frowned and shook his head. Tyler watched her retreating form, that still-perfect body. No woman he has ever known walked with such grace and unconscious sex appeal as Vena. His Vena; my God he'd missed her. Doesn't she know just how hot she is? Talk about aging well.

"Tyler, please take her home; better yet, take her to your place," Hanna whispered.

"I can't, not while she's been drinking," Tyler declared.

The girls frowned, "Excuse me, slightly inebriated," they each said and laughed.

"Go ahead, Tyler," Mary chimed in and Dee agreed.

"If it eases your mind, we trust you, and Vena trusts you," Hanna added. "But believe this, if you abuse her, hurt her or use her, there will be hell to pay," she warned.

Tyler took a step back, believing what she said, and responded thoughtfully. "I love her too," Tyler stated firmly and looked directly at Vena, who was deep in conversation with a server and trying hard to look abstemious. Tyler chuckled. His classy lady, he smiled.

Tyler looked at Hanna. "What about John?" he asked.

"Psssh, she got rid of that sorry Negro long ago," Hanna said earnestly. "But before he left, he broke her. She is just now getting her life back. She's been through hell and back, and we want her here with us; do you understand? She's an extraordinary person, you know."

"Yes, I know," he said, his eyes unwaveringly watching Vena.

"So," Hanna said, "take her home - yours, hers, who cares… just take her," Hanna added. "I'm drunk, horny, and sleepy.

The girls shook their heads, laughing.

Vena looked up and smiled, waving for them to come on.

"Go," each girl said at the same time.

"All right," he agreed. "See you later."

Tyler walked to Vena, who was leaning heavily on the wall of the solarium. When he stood before her, she took his hand. She smiled up at him. In the background, the melodic sounds of *Kenny G's Silhouette* cloaked the room in a romantic ambiance. "Oh, Tyler, I love this song," Vena said slowly.

"Dance with me, Vena," Tyler said, taking her hand and pulling her into his arms. She smelled of her favorite perfume, *Anais, Anais*. He pulled her into his arms and was not surprised at how well she fit in his arms. They swayed to the music, each privately savoring the moment. Hanna, Mary, and Dee waved as they walked out of the solarium. He smiled at them and then looked down at Vena.

"I missed you, Friend," she replied softly.

"Me too," he said, now realizing just how much.

She laid her head on his shoulder and closed her eyes. Tyler felt too right, smelled too good, and looked fantastic.

"You are still beautiful, Vena," Tyler whispered.

Slowly her head rose, and she looked at him.

"That's not true, Ty," she said, laying her head back on his shoulder.

"Still the same Vena," he replied and shook his head.

He pulled her closer. Tyler wondered about the kiss that she had given him when he had first walked in to her.

"Classy, why did you kiss me like that?" he asked.

She looked at him. She knew he was saying something, but she just melted into his dark brown eyes. Her stomach flipped, her heart pounded in her ears, and she felt something she had not felt for a long time, an undeniable desire she should not be feeling. Her hand slowly caressed his back. She pressed her body into him as she followed his every move while they danced. She stretched her head up and kissed him. He was startled at first but did not hesitate to return the kiss. He wanted to feel the moist heat of her mouth against his again. Gripping her head, he slanted his mouth over hers. He groaned when he felt her shudder; he then heard her purr soft and low in her throat and dragged his mouth away. He gazed down into her face. He never imagined she would taste this delicious.

"Tyler," she said softly against his lips, "I've missed you."

"Me too, Classy."

"Take me home," she whispered.

Together they walked out, his hand around hers as he gently guided her to the vehicle.

Chapter Two

It was a warm June night in Rockford. The stars twinkled brightly and the half-moon seemed brighter than usual.

He opened the door to his black Mercedes and helped her into the seat. Her head fell back against the headrest, and her eyes closed. After fastening her seatbelt, he took his place behind the wheel. "Are you okay?" he asked.

"Wonderful," she said, looking over at him and smiling with those perfect lips.

"Classy, where do you live?"

She lifted her head, leaned over and kissed him so passionately, his breath caught in his chest. She coaxed him with her mouth, telling him what she wanted. She pulled away slowly, and again rested her head and closed her eyes.

She spoke, "Nice car, Ty," without opening her eyes.

Vena's head was spinning and not only because of the champagne. It had to be Tyler. She never realized how much she missed him or how much she needed him. When she was going through all the drama of her life, she had wanted her friend with her. Many nights she cried and prayed for him to come for her. She wanted him to hold her and tell her everything was all right now. Nevertheless, he was here now, and it felt glorious to be with him again.

It amazed Tyler how forward Vena had become. She had never come on to him in such a way or even so much as flirted with him. It had to be the champagne. He had not realized how much he missed his girl until he saw her sitting so prim and proper in the solarium.

She was older, no doubt, with her hair pulled back in the bun that she always wore, but she was still as lovely. He had only seen her shoulder length hair down once, and it only added to her appeal. She didn't flaunt her sensuality; he didn't think she knew she had such unbelievable sex appeal. Vena still dressed immaculately and extremely conservative. Tyler reached over and lifted her hand to his lips. She smiled, never opening her eyes. He pulled into his condominium parking space. He was taking her to his home. *Then what?* He wanted her, there was no doubt about that, but he would not seduce her. More importantly, their friendship still meant a lot to him, and he didn't want to lose that. He knew she trusted him still after all these years and that meant everything to him.

He put the car in park and turned to look over at her. Her eyes were still closed. Was she asleep? Her head rose, she leaned over, and as if to reassure him, she kissed him. My God, he was as nervous as some young boy on his first date. He'd had his share of women, and none of them made him feel so uncertain. He had to take control before she had him acting like some blithering idiot. He pulled away and spoke softly in his sultry baritone voice.

"You've got to stop that," he chuckled, getting out of the car.

She smiled and waited for him to open her door. When she stood, it was on wobbly legs, and he was there to steady her. Her hands rested on his chest. She spoke softly.

"Where were you? I needed you." Her eyes filled with tears.

"I'm here now," he replied. Tyler guided her into his spacious home that was decorated to the nines. Her eyes surveyed the space, admiration in her eyes.

"You never did anything small, Tyler. Your home is lovely."

She walked away, sat on the white leather sofa, and crossed her legs.

"You hungry?" he asked.

"No."

"Something to drink?"

She shook her head. "Come sit with me."

She was quiet for a second. "Where have you been, Tyler?" she asked.

Tyler sat beside her but not too close. He had to keep his distance because he couldn't stop imagining her beneath him. He knew by how slowly her hazel eyes blinked that she was still tipsy. He lifted her feet onto his lap, removed her shoes, and began to massage her feet.

"Tyler, where were you?" she repeated.

"Building my fortune," he replied quietly.

She smiled. "And it seems you have. Kiss me Tyler," she insisted.

Before he knew it, he had pulled her onto his lap. His lips covered hers, instantly loving the warm taste of her sweet mouth as it opened to welcome his tongue. Her arms slipped around his neck, and she absently stroked it. He groaned and intensified the kiss, loving her sighs as her chest pressed into him. He left her mouth and trailed kisses down her neck to her bare chest. Her head fell back. He paused, his breathing heavy and thick.

"Don't stop, Ty," she said breathlessly. "I've been waiting for you so long; please don't let me go."

Tyler sighed low in his throat and kissed her with a passion he never knew he had, and she met his kiss with the same intensity. She was small and so fragile in his arms. His grip loosened, and she held on tighter. He lifted her effortlessly, placing her on her feet.

Tyler whispered against her lips, "Do you want me, Vena?"

"Yes."

"If we do this, Vena, there will be no turning back, you understand," he stated.

"I've been waiting for you," she whispered. She looked at him with tear-filled eyes. The tears swelled and flowed onto her cheeks.

"I'm here now, Classy," he said, pulling out her hair so it framed her oval face. He lifted her, carried her to his bedroom, and gently laid her on the king-sized bed before lying beside her.

"Kiss me, Ty," Vena demanded. His mouth covered hers, tasting her and loving it.

Vena began unbuttoning his shirt. Before he raised his head, she had his shirt open. She pushed him onto his back and straddled him. She pulled her blouse over her head and tossed it to the floor. She sat on him in her lacy black bra with her long skirt bunched up around her hips. Her eyes stayed fixed on his face. Tears glistened in her eyes as she unhooked her bra and tossed it aside. Tyler's breath caught in his throat at the beauty of her full breasts. His eyes trailed down to her flat belly and her petite waist. Tyler wanted to touch her, to feel her soft body in his hand. Gingerly he cupped her breast. Vena moaned softly, and her eyes closed. She rose to pull his pants down. When did she unbuckle his pants? He had to get control back; he didn't even know when he had lost it. He flipped her to her back, and her eyes widened in surprise. He placed feather light kisses on her face, his mouth so gentle she could barely feel his lips on her. His mouth found her breasts. Gently, he sucked her already hardened nipples as his tongue flickered over the nipples. Vena sighed and arched her back. She pushed his shirt from his shoulders, feeling sinewy muscles under her hands. She ran her hand down his back to his buttock. He rose from her and removed her skirt.

Vena's eyes roamed over his body. *He is magnificent*, she thought, with his broad, muscular chest, hard flat stomach, and narrow hips blending down to long muscular legs. When completely nude, he joined her on the bed. Vena didn't realize she had been staring until their eyes met. Tyler kissed her, and then his mouth wandered to her breast and sucked her nipple until she felt she was going to pass out from the sheer joy of feeling his mouth on her. He trailed kisses down her flat stomach until he was between her legs. When she felt the heat of his breath, she sat quickly.

"No, Ty, I…" she began, startled.

"Let me taste you, baby," he said huskily. She eased to her back. He opened her up gently, and his tongue traced her inner folds slowly. Vena inhaled and held her breath, waiting for the next sensation. He licked the nub and pulled it into his mouth, sucking it until he could hear Vena pleading softly. He then pushed his tongue into her now moist opening. She clutched the sheets in her fists. She felt as if she were floating, reaching for something she needed desperately.

"Please, Tyler," she moaned. "I need, I'm …"

Tyler was above her, gently entering her. "You want this," he said. "So tight," he groaned.

She started to convulse around him and moved with a rhythm that was pulling him deeper inside her. She wrapped her legs around his waist and her arms around his body. He couldn't hold back anymore. She was tight, hot, and coming with his every stroke. Although he was above her, she rode him as if she were on top.

My God, he thought, if she didn't stop, he was going to lose control.

"Tyler, please," she begged, "I can't... I've never felt this way."

"Relax, Baby," Tyler coaxed as he slowed her down. "Don't fight it; let it happen."

She held onto him tightly. Tyler moved in and out of her slowly. He felt her body tense beneath him.

"Relax, baby. Go with it. Follow my body," he said soothingly. "That's it. Let me love you; let me stroke you. Yes, baby," he hissed. "Take all of me. Feel how hard I am for you."

She was so hot and wet. Her tight walls sporadically pulsed around him. He moved deeper inside her, unlocking her floodgates. When she clamped around his hardened manhood, her hot juices flowed, and he plunged deeper and harder, joining her as they both went over the edge.

She lay on her back with Tyler sprawled across her body. He could hear her soft, deep breathing. Never had he experienced lovemaking as intensely as what he'd just shared with Vena. Never would he have thought he and Vena would be this exceptional together. Tyler was still inside her, and she started to gyrate, instantly causing him to harden and grow. She rolled him onto his back. With her hands on his chest, she smiled ever so slightly. She rose and lowered on him. His hands caressed her breasts, gently massaging them. She was riding him so erotically. Slowly, Vena raised and lowered on him, and his hips met hers as strong sensations raced through her. She felt as if she were drowning and did not want to be rescued. She arched her back and was lost in the responsiveness of his body. He lifted her hips holding her above him so just a fraction of what he possessed was inside her. He rotated his manhood in her, pulling at her soul. She tighten around him, he sat her down on him, and they both accepted the zenith of their lovemaking. Trying to catch her breath, she folded over and rested her head on his shoulder.

"What are you doing to me, Ty? I can't move," she said in a muffled voice as her face was pressed into his neck.

"Excuse me, I didn't quite hear what you said," Ty replied with a smile.

"I can't move," she said and bit him playfully on his shoulder.

She took a shaky breath, "I've waited a long time for you to make love to me, and now I'm paralyzed," she moaned.

That struck Tyler so funny that he rolled her off him and sat up, laughing.

Vena frowned at him. "That's not funny, Tyler." Tyler could not stop laughing, maybe because he was happy.

"I'm leaving, Tyler. Stop laughing."

"Okay, I'm sorry." He started laughing again when he looked at her. She loved when he laughed; it was a glorious sound.

Vena frowned and rolled from the bed. Tyler caught her and pulled her back to bed.

"Stop it, Tyler. It is not that funny," she pouted.

"I've missed you, Classy," he said and kissed her forehead. She wrapped her arms around his neck.

"I waited for you, Ty," she said, raising her mouth to his.

He covered her mouth with no hesitation, and they made love again. Their lovemaking was so sweet and so meaningful that they were both in awe of the feeling they brought from each other.

Vena stretched like a well-satisfied cat when she awoke. She hadn't slept like that for years. Vena turned her head to look at Tyler. Good, he was still asleep. She pulled the sheet around her and slid off the oversized bed. The pulling of the sheet stopped her escape. "Where are you going?" Tyler asked with eyes still closed.

"Home," she teased. Tyler frowned, eyes snapping open.

"Home," he repeated, dumbfounded.

She snatched the sheet from him and went into the bathroom. Tyler lay back on his bed, a contented man with a wide, satisfied grin on his face. He was glad to have her back in his life. What if their lovemaking ruined their friendship? Tyler shook his head. He didn't want to think of *what ifs* or if the passion they shared would ruin that friendship. Tomorrow, they would deal with the rest. Sighing, Tyler lay with his hands behind his head, very satisfied. No woman has ever made love to him with the passion Vena had. Who would have thought that tiny body held all that passion? *There was no way Vena was going to be out of his life now that she was with him; not ever again*, he declared to himself. She will not only still be his best friend, but she will also be his woman.

He swung his legs over the side of the bed and looked at the bedside clock, reading 4 AM. Going to the bathroom, he heard the shower running. He eased open the door. Vena stood with her back to him in the glass-enclosed shower; water beads trailed down her shapely body. Tyler leaned in the doorway watching her. As if he willed it, she turned. Her eyes traveled the length of his beautiful body with a lustful smile on her face. Vena said softly, "Come here, and let me show you something."

Tyler smiled and shook his head.

"Come here," she purred.

Again, he shook his head. She shrugged her shoulder and turned her back to him letting the water cascade down her body. With her eyes closed, she allowed the hot water to soothe her. She knew Tyler was watching. Vena slowly and seductively began to soap her body moving her hand caressingly over her breast and to her stomach. When her hand reached the junction between her legs, she caressed herself unabashedly as if making love to herself. Her head fell back, letting droplets of water flow from her hair.

Tyler watched with an eager amusement. When she began to caress herself, his expression changed to yearning. He stepped into the shower and pulled her against him.

"You're not playing fair," he said huskily, nibbling on her ear.

Vena turned into his arms and began to lather his chest. Her hands trailed down his hard-velvety frame. Slowly, she soaped his body, rubbing her hands in a caressing circular motion on his chest and slowly lowering down his body until she held his member in her hands. She stroked him with gentle hands. She kissed his chest, her tongue touching his hard-pebbled nipples. Tyler moaned, and his eyes closed as he savored the feel of her hands on him. Her lips traveled down to his flat, muscular abdomen, feeling his muscles contract under her mouth. She moved lower until she replaced her hands with her mouth. A small moan eased from Tyler. Slowly her mouth moved up and down on him then released him to lick the length of his well-endowed member. She pulled the tip into her mouth and gently sucked on it, feeling him pulsate in her mouth.

Tyler stood still, allowing her to do to him as she pleased; never did he think she would feel this good. He growled and lifted her up with no effort. She straddled him, her legs circling around his waist, as he quickly slid inside her with his hand beneath her bottom.

"Yes," he whispered, pressing her back to the shower wall and taking control. Vena moaned and held onto him tight as his mouth covered hers in a heated mind shattering kiss. His tongue mimicked the way he moved inside her. He called out her name when the heat of her love poured down his shaft, causing him to explode within her. They stood entangled, breathing heavily and holding one another tightly. After a minute, Vena unfolded her legs while still breathing deeply and languidly rested her head on his chest. Barely recovered, Tyler caressed her sensitive body. Vena thought if she moved she was sure she would fall. She didn't have to. Tyler picked her up, wrapped her in a towel and carried her to his bed. He joined her and made love to her until they both fell into a sated and exhausted sleep in each other's arms.

Vena awoke suddenly, unsure of her whereabouts. Her stomach did a flip when she remembered the night's events, and she groaned softly. She looked over at the sleeping Tyler and gingerly rolled away from him, careful not to awaken him. Vena found the clothes she hastily discarded on the floor, dressed quickly, and quietly walked out his front door.

****

Tyler stretched with a leisurely smile on his handsome face. He rolled over. The side of the bed was empty.

"Classy?" he called. No answer.

"Classy?" he called louder in alarm. Frowning, he quickly rose from the bed. He instantly noticed her clothes were gone from the floor. He sat on the side of the bed, dejected and a little angry. "Damn it," he cursed.

Vena walked to the Corner Bakery. She pulled her phone from her purse and dialed.

"Hello?" a groggy, sleepy voice answered.

"Hanna," Vena said.

"Vena, what's wrong?" Hanna's voice alarmed.

"Can you pick me up?" Vena asked.

"Where's Tyler?" Hanna inquired.

"I left him home asleep."

"Where are you?"

"Northbrook Center at the Corner Bakery," she answered.

"I'll be right there," Hanna hung up.

What was I thinking ran through her mind? She fondly remembered his handsome face with his boyish feature. He looked terrific for 52; his dark skin was smooth, hard, and soft all in one. She could still feel his full, shapely mouth on hers, as she remembered how marvelous his mouth felt. The way he made love to her made her heart flutter wildly in her chest. Come back to reality, she told herself, come back. This will not happen again. My God, she acted like some brazen, hard-up hussy. What did he think of her? Moaning, Vena's hands covered her face. Would she be able to live this down?

Hanna arrived, "Vena, you okay?" Hanna asked as she rushed into the bakery. Vena nodded, rising to leave.

"What happened?" Hanna asked frantically, following her.

"Everything," Vena groaned.

As the car pulled from the parking lot, Vena silently stared blankly out the window.

"So?" Hanna coaxed after a few seconds. "What happened?"

"Hanna, what do you think?" she responded, not believing Hanna had asked her that.

"That bad, huh?"

"No, that good. Oh God, Hanna, was I drunk?" she asked, disgusted with herself.

"No, you were slightly inbre…"

"It's not funny, Hanna," she said with anguish. "I had him all night long, and I loved it." Vena sighed. "I never knew it could be… so... ah…"

"Fabulous," Hanna finished for her, laughing.

"Fabulous? That's putting it mildly," Vena said, still feeling the aftermath of their lovemaking.

Hanna laughed. "That's good; you have now experienced the best ..."

"Don't be so crass, Hanna," Vena scolded. Hanna laughed.

"Don't laugh, Hanna."

Hanna stopped laughing but continued to grin.

"I'm sorry. So now what, and why did you leave?" Hanna inquired.

"Scared, embarrassed, I don't know," Vena groaned, covering her face with her hands.

"Embarrassed?" Hanna repeated, her curiosity peaked.

Vena looked over at Hanna. "I'll never tell the things we did, so don't ask," she told her, meaning every word.

Hanna chuckled. "So, you just left him."

"Asleep," Vena finished.

"What?" Hanna laughed. "You really know how to make an exit. Did you at least leave your number?"

"Are you crazy," Vena said incredulously. "He might call, and again I'd be back in his bed."

"So, what's wrong with that?" Hanna inquired.

"I know Tyler. He loves women; he always has. Damn, look at him - and the women love him." Vena shook her head. "I can't risk getting involved with him that way; no, I can't do it," she said, shaking her head decisively.

Hanna pulled into Vena's driveway. Vena got out of the car and looked into the window at Hanna.

"What am I going to do, Hanna?" she asked.

"I know I just met your Tyler, but I think he is a genuine guy, and fine too. I think you're nuts if you let what happened affect you negatively. At least think about it, sweetie. Call me later," Hanna said before pulling from the driveway.

Vena walked up a flight of stairs to her loft above her dance studio. In a couple of hours, she would be conducting her beginner's dance class, and she had to have her faculties about her. She scolded herself enough thinking about Tyler Kinson and last night.

Chapter Three

Vena looked at the clock on the wall; she had a couple of hours before her next class. She'd use the time to work on some new choreography for the next recital. Searching through her cds, Vena came across Kenny G, and played the same song she and Tyler had danced to last night. She closed her eyes and could almost feel Tyler's arms around her. Tears filled her eyes and rolled slowly down her cheeks. Taking slow steps back to center floor, she did a double pirouette and reached forward, facing the studio mirror. Releve', arabesque, short run small leap, pirouette, reach, pas de bourree' battement' turn, arms wide.

"Beautiful," a familiar baritone voice said.

Stunned, Vena stopped and turned in the direction of that sultry voice she had never forgotten all those years. Tears streamed down her face, Vena turned from him. Tyler went quietly and stood close behind her.

"Classy," he whispered, "don't."

"Ty, I can't do this with …" she hiccupped.

"Why, baby?" He turned her to face him.

"I'm scared of this, afraid of you. I just can't risk it."

"Sh... it's okay," he said soothingly, pulling her into his arms.

Vena pulled away from him. "No, Tyler, we're friends. Even if we haven't seen each other for years, you are still my friend. I never stopped loving you as that friend. It means too much to me to complicate it with great sex. I don't want our friendship to end. We can't do this again," she stated adamantly.

"Classy, did you ever think this is the way it should be; maybe it was meant for me to see you last night," Tyler implored her.

Vena shook her head, "No Tyler!" Vena said firmly.

Tyler went to her, turning her to face him. He did not intend to let her out of his life ever again. He missed her friendship, and he didn't want to lose the love he knew they could share. He wasn't giving up on this; this was meant to be, and he knew it in his heart and soul.

"Vena, I know our friendship is important. We love each other. You will always be my best friend. You are the only woman I know that I can talk to about anything. Why can't it be more? Why can't we be more to each other? You have to know it's good, in and out of bed. I would cut my heart out before I would hurt or disappoint you in any way. You know that, don't you?" Tyler searched her face.

Tears seeped from her closed eyes and rolled down her face. Her eyes opened. She gazed at him, and he saw her beautiful eyes filled with fear and doubt. "I don't know if I can let my heart love that way ever again. I don't think I can love you the way you need to be loved."

"Classy? Did you enjoy me last night?" Tyler asked seductively.

Vena's heart fluttered. She nodded.

"I enjoyed you also. We are not getting any younger. I want you in my life, Classy—no, I *need* you in my life. Give us a chance. I know you can love me the way I need, and I know I can love you how you need to be loved. Do you want to try?"

Vena sighed. She could not help but smile. "Yes, I want to try."

Tyler pulled her into his arms. Slowly, her arms went around his neck, and she held him tightly as her heart rapped hard against her chest. He exhaled, relieved. He couldn't – no, he *wouldn't* let her go now that she was back in his life.

"Which way?" he asked.

He lifted her in his arms, close to his chest, and carried her to the bedroom in her loft.

"Tyler, what …?"

"Shh, I'm going to make you feel better." He laid her on the bed and undressed her. Then he made love to her, and she let him.

Tyler lay on the bed beside Vena and watched her sleep. She lay on her stomach with her head turned towards him and the sheet down around her waist. He is not going to risk losing her again. He admits when he found her gone, a slight panic coursed through him. He searched the phone book, found her address, and then came to see his soon to be lady. After kissing her cheek and covering her, he left.

Vena stretched and yawned languidly, glancing at the window and the darkened sky. Swearing, she sat up in her rumpled bed, kicking at the sheets that tangled around her legs. "Oh no, what time is it?" she cried aloud in a panic.

She jumped out of the bed naked. *Where is Tyler,* she wondered? She heard voices coming from downstairs. Pulling on her robe, she went down the circular staircase to her living room. There sat Tyler, Hanna and her latest Robert, Dee and her new man Cedric, and Mary and her husband Tom, laughing it up and having a grand time.

Tyler saw her first. "Hey, Classy," he greeted and went to kiss her. Vena put her hand over her mouth and his.

"What's going on?" she asked. "I had a class six hours ago."

"Oh," Hanna said, "didn't I tell you I canceled it?"

Vena shook her head, a frown on her face.

"Sorry, I forgot," Hanna shrugged, grinning.

"Hanna," she said, looking at her suspiciously. "What did you do?"

"Get dressed, Classy," Tyler interrupted. "I cooked."

"Only if you help me," she said crossly through clenched teeth. She pinched his arm, pulling him with her.

"Ow," she replied, but he followed her.

When they reached her bedroom, Tyler sheepishly replied, "You need to go the market; I had to get food to prepare for dinner." He hoped that changing the issue would help.

"Tyler, what are you doing?" she faced him.

"Being good to you," he replied proudly.

"By canceling my class?!" she yelled.

"I didn't do that; Hanna did," he said, sounding like a boy putting the blame on his sibling.

"I think you and those girls' downstairs are in cahoots." She walked into the bathroom.

"Still need my help, Classy?" Tyler sighed with relief, glad he was no longer in trouble.

"No," she said and slammed the bathroom door.

Tyler smiled. Canceling her class was not his idea. He just happened to answer the phone while she slept. It was Hanna, Dee, and Mary on three-way, and Tyler reported she had been upset when he found her in the studio. He explained to the girls that they decided to give their relationship a chance. That's when Hanna told him that she would cancel Vena's last class so they could all get together, which he was all for. He wasn't willing to let Vena go. The sad thing about it all is it took him ten years to realize he needed her in his life. They were happy together, and not just in bed. They've always had a lot in common. She was his friend first, but he was determined to make her his woman now. He knew she had been through something; what, he didn't know, but he would be patient and wait until she wanted to talk about it.

"Need me to wash your back, Classy," he called through the closed door.

"No!" she snapped. "Go entertain your guests!"

Twenty minutes later, Vena joined them. Everyone quieted when she entered the room. Tyler brought her an apple martini; she took it and rolled her eyes at him.

"This is my last drink," she announced.

Everyone in the room exhaled and started to laugh when Vena couldn't help herself and joined in.

"We did it because we love you, and you needed it, the rest I mean," Hanna said, grinning at the double meaning not missed by the girls. Everyone laughed; embarrassed,

Vena still smiled. They ate, played cards, and talked. Overall, the evening turned out to be fun, something Vena had not had in a long time. Everyone liked Tyler, and that made her happy. She wanted her closest friends to like him. Maybe there was more to the relationship between Tyler and her than she could see right now.

About 11 PM, everyone left. Hanna hugged her. "Keep him, girl," she whispered.

"You did well," Dee said.

"You're glowing, Sweetie, don't lose it," Mary said.

Then they were alone. Vena stood against the door.

Tyler stood, trying to look innocent.

"What?" he said and smiled.

She walked slowly towards him. He took a step back.

"I had forgotten how charming you could be. How did you get the girls to scheme with you? Lucky for you, mister, they like you."

She kept advancing. He backed up.

"Are you angry?" he asked.

"Yes!" she stated firmly.

"How can I make it all better?"

Straight-faced, she said, "Take off your clothes."

"What?"

"Now!"

She was still approaching him as he was taking steps backward.

He frowned, confused. "What?" He stopped in front of the chair.

Vena pushed him into the chair. She got down on her knees and began to undo his belt.

"What are you doing, Miss?"

"Shh…" she said and picked up the remote, lowered the lights, and pressed another button for Babyface to begin to play on the stereo. Tyler tensed in the chair, not knowing what to expect. Vena released him from his pants and kissed him. Her tongue circled him. She pulled him into her mouth. Tyler's head fell back against the chair, savoring her mouth on him. Vena could hear the faint moans that escaped his lips. Tyler pulled her up easily from the floor to straddle his hips. He lifted her skirt, moved her underwear aside, and entered her. She was wet for him. How could that be when she was the one pleasuring him? He held her as she sank down on his rock hard shaft and gripped him tightly inside her hot, wet body.

"You want me," he stated huskily, loving the feel of her on him.

"I've wanted you all night," Vena sighed. "Stay with me tonight, Tyler."

Vena awoke, still spooned with Tyler. It's Sunday; she had to get dressed or be late for church. Vena tried gently removing herself out of his arms without waking him, but he pulled her back against him.

"Where are you going?" he whispered in her ear. She turned to him.

"You're awake," she smiled.

"I've been awake for a while, just lying here loving the feel of you in my arms and not wanting to leave you."

Vena returned his smiled. She felt the same way, but it was time to get back to reality. She lay there just looking at him. How many times had she wanted Ty, needed Ty, just to talk to him about things? If he were still in her life when John…. The thought of that monster made her tremble with fear. Her body tensed. Tyler felt the change in her body. She rolled away from him and sat up on the side of the bed. *Not now,* she told herself, don't remember what John did to you now.

She visibly trembled. Tyler reached out to touch her. Vena pulled away.

"Hey, what's wrong?" Tyler rose up on his elbow with a frown on his handsome face.

"Nothing," she said, getting up and going to the bathroom. Tyler followed her. He grabbed hold of her arm and turned her around. Her eyes widened, and she pulled away, obvious fear on her face. Tyler frowned, not understanding what was happening. He pulled her into his arms and held her close. Vena buried her face in his chest. She was holding on to him tightly. "I needed you, Ty; I needed you," she said against his chest.

He lifted her head. "What happened to you, baby? Tell me," he insisted.

"I can't talk about this right now. Make me forget, Ty," she told him and began to kiss him on his bare chest.

Chapter Four

Vena sat on the floor of the studio stretching. Her chest lay on the floor, and her legs were astride. She tried hard not to dwell on Tyler, but he was all that was on her mind lately. After he had left Sunday morning, she hadn't seen or heard from Tyler. Was truly what they shared a weekend fling, and had he moved on already?

Maybe, Ty didn't want the relationship they spoke of after all. She could accept that. She didn't want any emotional involvement with any man, not even Ty. She smiled. It was a fantastic weekend. Still feeling the effects of Tyler's lovemaking, she sighed. Her face heated when she recalled how brazen and bold she was during their lovemaking. He brought something out in her she never knew she had. Vena knew she would never forget those moments in her mind for a long time. She was still lying on the floor, when Hanna, Dee, and Mary arrived. Every Monday was studio business, including discussing upcoming events.

"Vena, girl did you hear me?" Hanna asked.

"Huh? I'm sorry," Vena replied.

"Having flashbacks," Hanna teased. They all laughed.

"I don't kiss and tell," Vena joked.

"Yes, you do," they all said in unison and laughed.

"I don't any more," she laughed.

"Hey, we like Tyler. He's a great guy," Dee said.

"Yes, he is," Vena agreed.

"Have you heard from him today?" Mary asked.

"No, not since Sunday morning," she shrugged.

"You okay with that?" Hanna asked with concern in her voice.

"Yeah, it's okay if I never hear from Ty again. I'll never forget this past weekend," she said with a swooning sigh.

The buzzer rang at the studio door. "I'll get it," Dee called. Dee came back carrying two dozen yellow roses.

"My goodness," Hanna and Mary said as Vena's mouth dropped open.

"They're from Tyler, I know it," Dee said proudly. Vena's smile widened.

"There's a card," Dee said, handing it to Vena.

Hey Classy

Had to go to Rockford; problems with restaurant. I'll be back Friday.

Call me, 501-721-1277.

Had a great weekend. Can we have another?

Tyler

"Didn't I tell you he's the one?" Hanna bragged.

"So how do you feel about this? It is clear that he cares about you," Mary stated.

"Of course he cares; we were friends first," Vena replied.

"And now lovers," Hanna added. "Why fight it? I think you deserve a man like Tyler, Vena. Just let whatever happens, happen."

"You're right. I'm just going to enjoy whatever we have now," Vena decided.

"Good," they all chimed in.

Vena held the phone receiver to her ear waiting for Tyler to answer.

"Hello," Tyler said.

"Thanks for the roses; they're beautiful," she said.

"I hope they are still your favorite," Tyler replied.

"They are. Thank you."

"I'd like to take you somewhere Friday evening when I get back. Are you free?"

"Yes, where are we going?"

"Can I surprise you?" Tyler asked.

"If you want," she answered.

"Tomorrow you will receive a package from Fed-Ex. Just be ready Friday by 7 PM, okay?"

"All right, I'll be ready, Tyler. Give me a hint?" she asked.

"The only hint I have is that you will love the surprise," Tyler answered with a chuckle.

"Are you sure?" Vena asked.

"I know you will. See you Friday," he said and hung up the phone.

Tyler sat at his desk, very proud of himself. He picked up the phone and called Hanna, leaving her a message to call him without Vena.

Later that day, he had a three-way call with the girls. He explained to them his surprise for Vena. He had to make them a part of her surprise because they were pivotal in Vena's life. The girls were thrilled. Tyler knew if anyone could pull it off, the girls could. He was satisfied.

****

Vena stood in front of the full-length mirror in awe. She never thought she could be this beautiful. Hanna, Dee, and Mary stood behind her, grinning like idiots. The Fed Ex package Tyler sent was a beautiful Oscar De La Renta halter gown. It was white with gold throughout the fabric. The back of the gown dipped down past her waist, leaving her back bare except for the two thin straps crossed on her back. The front plunged modestly between her breasts. A matching shawl completed the gown. On her feet, she wore gold-strapped sandaled heels. Her hair she chose to wear in loose curls around her shoulders because Tyler requested it. If the glow on her face were any indication, she felt beautiful. He also supplied her with a pair of diamond-studded earrings and a diamond bracelet. Leave it to Tyler to think of everything. Vena felt like a schoolgirl going to her first prom. Never has she felt this lovely in all her life. It made her wonder where Tyler was taking her in all this finery.

"Girl, you look so good," Hanna cooed. Mary and Dee nodded their agreement. Vena smiled. These ladies were the only family she had other than her two adult children, and they stuck by her even after the damage John had done to her. Closing her eyes and taking a deep breath, she hated that she could think of him at a time when she should be happy. Not tonight, she told herself. Tonight is a happy time and nothing was going to ruin it, not even the unpleasant memories of the past. Hanna, the mother hen of the three women, noticed the change in Vena's demeanor.

"Hey, Vee, you okay?" Hanna asked with concern.

"I'm fine; I'm just thinking about how you all stuck with me and took care of me. I love you girls so much for being my family," she said, a little choked up.

"Stop thinking about that," Mary ordered. "We know you love us, and we love you too."

"Yeah," Dee added. "This is your special night. John will be in jail for a very long time, and he can't hurt you now."

"I know, I know," Vena agreed.

"Tyler's back in your life, and we know he really cares about you, Vee," Hanna replied. Before Vena could respond, the doorbell rang.

Vena smiled, excitement coursing through her. "He's here."

"I'll let him in," Mary announced. Dee and Hanna followed behind her. Vena heard their voices below, instantly recognizing Tyler's baritone voice. She smiled nervously, taking one last look at herself in the mirror. If she weren't floating, she certainly felt as if she were. Tyler stood in the living room with Mary, Dee, and Hanna. Vena stopped in the middle of the staircase and gazed at Tyler. She always thought Tyler was a handsome man, but tonight he was breathtaking, decked out in his Navy Armani suit. Exhaling a deep breath, she continued slowly down the staircase.

Tyler's heart skipped a beat when she appeared. She was a vision to behold. Not realizing he was moving, he met Vena at the last step. Taking her hand, he raised it to his lips.

"You are so beautiful," he uttered softly.

"So are you," she replied, smiling.

Outside, a limo waited for them. They waved and left.

Holding her hand, Tyler said after they got into the car, "I want to kiss you so badly,"

"Then kiss me," she said. His lips touched hers softly. "Where are we going?" she asked.

"You'll see. I will tell you this: your surprise is in Chicago."

He poured a glass of Dom, which had been chilling in the car, and handed it to her. Vena watched him, a smile of pure contentment on her face.

"Tyler," she asked, "why are you doing this?"

"You deserve this, Classy," he replied, taking her free hand in his. "Let me put it this way. I didn't realize how much I missed you until I saw you. You were always on my mind, and I thought about you more times than I can count, as well as wondered how you were. But something is different about you; something happened. You don't have the fire in your eyes you had long ago," Tyler concluded. Vena pulled her hand away.

"See, what I mean?" He pulled her hand back into his.

"Something happened. I know you, Classy. I'm a patient man, when you're ready, you will talk to me." he said and brought her hand to his lips.

As they rode in luxury, they laughed and talked about the times they had shared in Chicago. Vena just hoped Tyler wouldn't bring up John; she wasn't willing to share that shame with him.

The car finally came to a stop. Vena looked out the smoky windows and could see other elegantly dressed people milling about outside.

"We're here," Tyler announced, smiling.

Vena exhaled and then smiled. "Okay, I'm ready."

The driver opened the door, Tyler slid out of the car, and Vena placed her small hand in his as he helped her from the car. She stood beside him, and the cameras started flashing as they walked on the red carpet to the theater. Vena looked up at him, smiling with wonder and joy. He smiled down at her as she held on to his arm tightly. It was all so overwhelming to her. A reporter stopped them.

"Tyler Kinson, well-known restaurateur. Hello, Mr. Kinson," the reporter spoke. "Being a principal supporter of the arts and sponsor of the Shadanco dance troupe, you must be saddened that this will be their last performance."

Tyler responded with the professionalism she knew he possessed. He spoke eloquently and with pride. She couldn't help being so proud of him. Many of Tyler's acquaintances, all of obvious means, greeted them. The elite of Chicago and well-known entertainers all came out to support Tyler's endeavor. Vena was introduced to a flurry of people who welcomed and accepted her. As the evening wore on, Tyler and Vena were separated. Tyler was on one side of the theater lobby watching Vena adapt to her surroundings. She was a charming and classy woman, and he was intensely proud to have her at his side. Right at that moment as he observed her, Tyler realized immediately that he was in love with Vena. Why, after ten years, did he not know that he was in love with her? He had always loved her. People they had worked with in the past always thought they were a couple back then. They'd always been just friends. He never made any romantic jesters towards Vena nor had she to him. Now it was different. After the realization of loving her, his determination was to win her love. Tyler smiled as he watched her talking with one person or the other. Her head turned and their eyes met from across the room. She graciously excused herself and walked towards him. He loved the way she glided through the groups of patrons. He also didn't miss the other men's admiring glances as she moved gracefully to him.

Tyler had been talking to the grand dame of the theater, Madame Evelyn Thurston. Madame, as she has been known to close friends, was an older, truly elegant, and extremely wealthy lady that had been an ardent admirer of Tyler. He was enthralled with Vena across the room, all conversation stopped.

Madame smiled, noticing the now-silent Tyler devouring that lovely woman with his eyes.

When Vena reached him, she placed her hand gently on his arm. He took her hand and tucked it around his elbow.

"You okay?" he asked, looking at her with all the love inside him. Vena looked up at him, and her eyes portrayed the same love from long ago. Smiling, she nodded,.

Madame noticed the exchange and smiled.

"Hello, young lady," Madame replied haughtily.

"Vena, this is my very good friend, Madame Evelyn Thurston. Madame, this is Vena Thorn," Tyler introduced proudly.

Vena extended her hand. "It's so nice to meet you," Vena said sincerely.

Madame gave Vena a thorough once over, looking over her horn-rimmed glasses. She prided herself on her ability to assess people and was an exceptionally fair judge of character. She also prided herself on the wisdom that came with age and living life. Just by looking at this Vena, she could see why Tyler was in love with her. Vena Thorn was a beautiful woman with very kind eyes.

"Yes, dear, it's nice to meet you also," Madame said, taking her hand.

Tyler smiled. If the Madame liked you, you were accepted into her circle, and everyone wanted to be accepted by Madame Thurston.

"You've done well this time, Ty. I like her," she whispered. The Madame was still holding on to Vena's hand, when she noticed this superfluous, gaudy woman coming their way.

Madame leaned toward Vena and whispered, "Here comes that gold digging Beverly in her *I-have- nothing-to-hide* gown."

Vena looked over the attractive woman coming towards them.

"Hello, Tyler," she cooed and kissed him on his lips, "Ms. Thurston and …"

"Vena Thorn," Tyler supplied. "Classy, this is Beverly Gaines."

Beverly had wanted Tyler for a long time, but she just couldn't seem to capture his interest. Beverly looked over at Vena. How could she not notice her? Everyone in the room was all abuzz about the woman who strolled in with the ever-popular Tyler Kinson. She had to admit this Vena was pretty.

"Hello, Vena. So you're Tyler's new flame?" she said cattily.

"No, I'm an old flame, just relit," Vena said, smiling sweetly.

Madame cleared her throat to suppress her amusement. Tyler's brows rose, and mischief shone in his eyes.

Beverly smiled tightly, hating Vena. "Oh, I must go. There's someone I must speak to." Then she was gone.

"I knew I would like her," Madame chuckled, leaving them.

"Sorry, Ty. It's obvious she has laid claim to you," Vena replied sheepishly.

"And you just can't have that?" Tyler inquired, grinning.

Vena's eyes lowered. "Not tonight anyway," she said softly. Tyler was a little disappointed by her answer.

The lights blinked, indicating the show was about to start.

"This way, Mr. Kinson," the attendant said and led them to the theater box.

The seating was excellent, giving them a full view of the entire stage. They were seated along with Madame Thurston and her companion. Excitement coursed through Vena as the curtain rose. She gasped when she saw the company of dancers perform excellent creative pieces. The dancers, the music, and the choreography were superb. Vena couldn't help but be impressed. Every step was done with skill and perfectly executed. She didn't know where this company originated from. She thought she knew every active dance company performing. Vena scanned through the program for any history on the dance company, but she found nothing, just headshots of the dancers.

Tyler glanced over at Vena to see her reaction to the dance troupe. The joy on her face when the curtain opened overwhelmed him. He had hoped, no prayed, she would love her surprise because it had only just begun. Mary, Dee, and Hanna, his conspirators, should now be in the audience and would meet up with Vena at the after party. He loved to see joy on Vena's face, and no one would convince him it wasn't fate that brought him back into Vena's life. Everything just seemed to fall into place.

Tyler knew of this dance troupe for years and was their largest contributor. A few months ago, the artistic director of the company came to him and inquired if he knew of someone interested in continuing the company after he retired. At the time, he didn't. When Vena mentioned that she wanted a dance company, everything fell into place. It had only taken him a matter of hours to acquire the troupe for Vena and fulfill her dream. Tyler was confident that Vena would run the company successfully, and with the help of Mary, Dee, and Hanna, she couldn't lose.

When intermission began, she looked over at Tyler and took his hand.

"Thank you so much for this, Ty. It is so wonderful. I love it." Tyler smiled at her.

"What is the name of this company?" she asked. "I would really like to meet the dancers and the director." She paused, looking over at Tyler. "Can I meet them?"

"Slow down, Baby. Yes, you'll be able to meet them all," he said. "Come, let's go for a walk. We need to talk to you."

Vena frowned, "What's wrong?"

"Nothing's wrong, Baby. Come."

Tyler found a secluded spot in the lobby.

"What is it, Tyler? You're scaring me."

"I need to tell you something."

"You're leaving," she interrupted.

"No, no, Classy," Tyler paused, "This Company is yours."

Vena was silent for a minute.

"What do you mean--your company?" she asked, stunned and confused.

"Your company," he said, smiling.

Vena looked at him astounded.

"How, Tyler, is this my company?" She paused. "You mean this is my company?" she said, placing her hand on her chest. "How?"

"Baby," he soothed, "it's yours. I acquired this company for you, to direct anyway it pleases you. The former artistic director and owners are retiring and didn't want to disband the troupe. When you mentioned you wanted to start a dance company, and being a major supporter of Shadanco, I made some calls, and here it is, Baby, your dream."

"Tyler," Vena was moved. Tears shone in her eyes. "Tyler, I'm speechless. Thank you just doesn't seem to express what I'm feeling at this moment," she whispered, overwhelmed with love for him as her arms wrapped around him.

She released him, and looked at him inquiringly.

"How did they put on the extravaganza without a director?"

"They've been rehearsing this past week, creating just for you. They are all looking forward to meeting their new Artistic Director."

"Oh, Ty, why did you do this? I love it." She hugged him again.

"Look at me, Classy," he said earnestly. "I did it to assure you that I believe in your dreams, just as you believed in me, and to show you how much I love…"

"Mr. Kinson, the show is about to continue," he was interrupted by the usher.

Tyler nodded, took Vena's hand, and returned to the theater box for the second act.

"Tyler, my heart is full." Tyler beamed at her.

They watched the rest of the performance in silence, the realization of it all hitting her. Tears of joy flowed down her face. When the show ended, the nine female dancers and nine male dancers took their bows, receiving a standing ovation. Even though it was a small group, the audience seemed to enjoy the performance. Every one of them was a talented dancer, and Vena was proud to be a part of her newly acquired dance company. She couldn't wait to get started.

Tyler leaned close to her and whispered, "This is all for you, Classy." Vena's hand went to her chest, as tears of joy spilled down her face. The spotlight then shone on her, and Vena stood and curtsied to her dancers. Cheers arose from the audience.

Tyler and Vena arrived at the hotel ballroom at the Chicago Ritz-Carlton, and the guests applauded. Vena was surprised when she saw Mary and Tom, Dee and Cedric, and Hanna and Robert. Vena looked over at Tyler, who was smiling proudly. The girls rushed over to hug her.

"You knew all the time," she accused the girls.

"Yes, isn't it a great surprise?" Hanna beamed with delight. Vena hugged her again.

"Go see your dancers, Vee. They're excited and looking forward to meeting you."

With her friends in tow, Vena made her way through the throng of people. She was congratulated, given best wishes, and received promises of support as she made her way to her dancers. Vena was thrilled. Her dream had actually come true, and Tyler was the reason for it. She stopped to embrace Madame.

"Tyler has truly outdone himself," Madame Thurston said, hugging her. "And what a beautiful celebration. You can expect my support and the support of my constituents."

"Thank you, Madame. Your acceptance of this company means so much to me." They embraced again, and Madame promised to keep in touch.

The dancers had heard so many positive things about Vena and were thrilled to meet her. She invited them all to Northbrook to establish plans for the company, encouraging their input. Again, Vena praised the dancers' performances and looked forward to working with them. Tyler joined her, also congratulating the dancers. Excusing them, Tyler took her hand and brought it to his lips, causing delicious shivers to race up her spine. He then led her from the group of dancers. Vena smiled as she gazed into his eyes.

"Mary, Dee, and Hanna retired for the evening. They're staying over and wanted to take advantage of the beautiful hotel suites; Hanna's words, not mine," he said. "I know you're tired. We have a suite upstairs also. Care to join me?"

Vena smiled. "Yes."

After saying goodnight to everyone, Vena and Tyler left for the elevator. Once alone, Tyler pulled Vena into his arms.

"I want you so bad," he whispered, his mouth near hers.

"Me too," her lips pressed to his. They were so into each other, they didn't notice the elevator doors had opened. Someone that had entered cleared his throat, only then did they pull apart.

"Sorry," Tyler apologized, pulling an embarrassed Vena against his side. Finally, the elevator doors opened to his floor. They quickly headed to the suite let her enter.

"Tyler," Vena said, turning to face him, "I don't know what to say about all you've done tonight."

"You've already stated it, but right now I want your clothes off. I need to be inside you very badly."

Vena smiled and turned her back to him. Tyler unzipped her gown and let it fall and puddle around her feet. Stepping from her gown, she turned to Tyler in her matching bra and thong panties and eased his jacket from his shoulders. She was so beautiful and sexy. She loosened his tie and began to unbutton his shirt. Tyler stood with his eyes shut, loving the feel of her small hands on him. Then it hit him hard. *I love this woman more than I ever thought I could love one person.*

When she had his shirt loose, he pulled her into his arms with a little more force than he intended and kissed her deeply. The moment his mouth covered hers, a flood of heated passion took over, consuming her. She held on to him and took all he was giving. Red-hot sensations filled her already sensitive body. Her arms wrapped around his neck as she pressed her throbbing body into his.

Tyler pulled his mouth away. "I've got to have you now," he murmured.

He lifted her and carried her to the bed. He laid her gently on the bed and pulled off her shoes. Lowering to his knees, he kissed the inside of her thigh with soft butterfly kisses. He was hungry for her taste. He pulled and ripped the thongs from her then tossed them across the room. In a smooth motion, he lowered his head and pulled her into his mouth as his eager tongue went straight to her core. His fingers parted her folds, and his tongue sank deeper inside her. A new sensation surged through him. He lifted her legs over his shoulders and fed on her honey greedily.

Vena screamed his name in sheer joy of what his mouth was doing to her. She shuddered and moved frantically beneath his mouth. He grasped her hips to hold her still as he brought her to a climax. He rose never taking his eyes off her, and watched her embrace her orgasm. It was a beautiful sight to see.

Vena's eyes opened, and her breath caught in her chest. She sensed a fierceness and determination in his body. Vena moved to the center of the bed while he removed his clothing. He joined her, his kiss robbing her of her breath. Vena noticed the change in Tyler; she wondered what was going on in his head. Slowly, he slid into her juicy body. Tyler leaned up while looking down at her. His arms, with muscles bulging, were on either side of her shoulders. He moved inside her as if he was in search of something. The more he searched, the more Vena moved beneath him; moving to a rhythm he had never experienced. His eyes closed and he savored the sensations that she gave him. What was she doing to him? His body stiffened. The more she gyrated beneath him, the more his control left him.

"Vena," he said huskily, "Please, baby, not yet."

Vena felt the same emotions with each movement he made. She felt him sink deeper inside her. "Tyler," she said breathlessly.

Each fought for their own sensations, pleasuring one another and pulling something deep from the other. They climaxed, but this time was different from the other times. Tyler felt he had planted his seed into her soul, and she had given hers.

"I love you, Classy," he spoke, his voice soft. "I've been in love with you for a very long time; I can't lose you this time."

Tears filled Vena's eyes. "I'm in love with you too. I think we have loved each other for a long time, and now fate has brought us together." Tears rolled down the sides of Vena's face. He kissed her.

"You are my life, Classy," he declared.

Vena wrapped her legs around his waist. "You're mine now, Ty. I'll never let you go again," she vowed.

All night they pleasured each other, basking in their newfound love for one another.

Next morning, Vena stretched, feeling euphoric. Right away, she felt the emptiness in the bed. She searched for Tyler and found him sitting at a table with covered dishes.

"You're awake," Ty announced, smiling. "Come have brunch." Vena rose and slipped on the hotel robe. She sat at the table, gazing at Tyler lovingly.

"So now what, Ty? Where do we go from here?" Vena asked.

"What do you mean?" he frowned.

"I love you, Tyler Kinson."

"Yes, Classy, I know," he smiled.

"Don't tease me, Ty. I need to know what happens now," Vena pouted.

"I love you, Classy. I always have, and I always will. Now we just love and take care of each other, and everything will fall into place."

"You promise?"

"With all my heart, Baby."

Chapter Five

Her troupe of dancers sat on the floor in her studio discussing the details of the new company. Hanna, Dee, and Mary were taking care of the administrative duties and informed the dancers about living arrangements and studio rehearsals. Everyone was excited and ready to get started on the première for Vena Thorn Dance Troupe in six months. Vena sat at the desk, going through the mail. She noticed an unopened letter from the state parole board. Why would she be getting a letter from the parole board? Not thinking much of it, she ripped the letter open and began reading it. She stared at the letter, still not comprehending at first. She reread it.

"No, no!" she screamed, alerting the others. "This can't be true," she cried in dismay while staring at the letter. She began to tremble violently as tears filled her eyes. Hanna rushed over to her and took the letter from her hand.

Vena was suddenly terrified. "I can't stay here; I have to leave!" She started pacing from one end of the office to the other, in no direction.

"My God, help me. He is going to come after me. I have to pack," she cried frantically.

Mary hugged her, trying to calm her. Dee reassure the alarmed dancers that witnessed Vena's outburst.

Vena pulled away and ran to her loft, Mary behind her. She didn't stop until she was up the staircase and in her bedroom. She pulled out her luggage and started throwing anything in it.

"Help me get away!" she shouted to Mary. Dee was still unaware of what was going on when she and Hanna joined them upstairs. They found Mary holding on to a visibly shaken Vena.

"My God, she's terrified," Mary said. "Hanna, what's going on?"

"John was released from prison as of last week. This letter is from the parole board."

"No, that can't be," Dee said. "I thought he had ten years."

"I called the parole board and spoke to the man assigned to him. Evidently, John's been an exemplary inmate, so they gave him early parole for his good behavior," Hanna replied sardonically.

The girls closed in, trying to calm her, but that only made her more hysterical. She pleaded with them to take her away.

"He said he would kill me next time. You were in court when he threatened me!" she shouted. "He'll find me here. Help me pack, please Hanna. Please, Mary help me."

"Dee, call Tyler," Hanna told her.

"We have to give her an injection, Hanna. She's hysterical," Mary told her, her nursing knowledge taking over.

"Should we?" Hanna asked. "You know how she hates that medicine."

"The doctor said if she should become overexcited, we have to calm her. We don't want her to have an anxiety attack. We'll call the doctor after I've given her the shot," Mary stated.

Mary retrieved the medicine from the bathroom. Each girl knew that Vena was very fragile when it came to her assault five years ago.

"Hanna, please don't call Tyler. He doesn't know about this. I don't want him to know." She pressed her face into Hanna's shoulder, crying heart-wrenching sobs while Hanna held her close.

"He won't want me if he knew the things John did to me."

"Shh… Shh… Vena, Tyler loves you. He will understand," Hanna attempted to reassure her. Mary had returned with the medicine.

"No, I'm afraid I will lose him if he knows," she cried.

Vena pulled away from Hanna and started to pace the floor, pulling her hair from its ponytail.

"God, I feel so dirty," she fretted. She began pulling off her clothes. Hanna rushed to her and tried to comfort her, but she pulled away and ran to the shower. Everything was coming back to her in a rush, as fresh as the day John assaulted her.

"Vee, it's going to be alright," Hanna's voice trailed behind her.

Vena stood under the shower scrubbing her body relentlessly with a cloth.

Hanna felt so helpless seeing Vena tormented with memories of what John Matthews had done to her. She couldn't forget how tormented Vena was when she first released from the hospital. The girls alternately stayed with her through the nightmares and depression. During that time, when things got their worst, she'd asked them why he didn't just kill her. She felt she couldn't live with this in her head. Nevertheless, she did, and the girls made sure of it. When Tyler came into her life, she was her old self. Now this.

"Vee," Hanna called, "Come out, Sweetie."

"I can't, not yet. I'm still so dirty." Tears filled Hanna's eyes. She turned away just when Tyler came barreling into the bedroom.

"What's happened?" Tyler asked sternly.

Hanna pointed to the bathroom. He saw Vena scrubbing herself roughly and vigorously washing her hair. Tyler turned to Hanna and the girls for answers. Vena was still unaware of Tyler's arrival.

"Why can't I get clean?" she yelled frantically.

"What happened?" Tyler asked abruptly

"Tyler, please, you have to help her," Hanna said. "You don't know what John did to her." Hanna handed him the letter from the parole board. He read it.

Confusion creased his brow.

"We have to get her to take a shot," Hanna told him.

"She needs to calm down before she hurts herself," Mary said anxiously.

"A shot," Tyler repeated confused. "What did he do to her?"

"I'll explain later. See if you can get her out of the shower."

Tyler didn't know what to expect, but he loved this woman with all his heart and would do anything to help her. Tyler entered the bathroom.

"Classy," he called calmly.

When Vena saw him, she became more agitated.

"No— No, Tyler, go away. I don't want you here. Please go," Vena pleaded.

"Baby, come out and let me help you."

"It's too late, Tyler, too late!" she yelled. "Get out! Get out!"

"Vena, I'm not leaving. I love you, Classy. Let me help you."

She turned to look at Tyler. He wasn't there before but he is now, she realized. She knew in her heart that he would keep her safe.

Vena turned off the water, and pressed herself against the wall of the shower, she cried despairingly. Tyler grabbed a towel, wrapped it around her shivering body, and led her from the shower. She stood while Tyler dried her. Someone handed him a gown, and as a child would, she stood while he dressed her.

Mary came to her. "Come, Vee, take the shot," she coaxed.

"No, please, I can't take that. I have to be aware," she replied adamantly.

"How can you touch me, Tyler?" she demanded.

"I love you!" he replied, knocked off balance by her outburst.

"No, Tyler, you don't love me. If you did, you would have come for me. I needed you, and I couldn't find you!" she screamed at him. She hit him and pushed him away.

Vena turned to Hanna. "Why didn't he just kill me? I would be better off. I can't live like this," she yelled and backed away from them.

Tyler went to her and pulled her into his arms. Vena tried to pull away, but Tyler held her close, soothing her with gentle words.

"I'm here now, Classy," he whispered. She looked up at Tyler, and the fog seemed to lift.

"Oh, Tyler," she cried, "I'm sorry. I didn't mean what I said…" and she began to weep. Tyler lifted her in his arms and sat with her on his lap. She curled against his chest like a child. He soothed her with soft words, as Mary administered the shot. Hanna indicated they would be downstairs before they left them alone.

Tyler held on to Vena tightly, tears filling his eyes. He hated seeing her like this. What did John do to break her like this, he wondered?

"Tyler, if you don't want me anymore," she slurred, "I understand." The medication quickly took effect. When her head fell to his shoulder, Tyler put her in the bed.

"Tyler, I love you. I always did; I always will," she whispered with eyes closed.

"I'm not going anywhere, Classy," Tyler promised and gently kissed her forehead.

Soon Tyler joined the other's downstairs. Hanna handed him a brandy, and he drank the fiery liquid in one swallow. He sat down heavily, his head lowered in defeat. He could tell by the looks of concern on their faces that he was not going to like what he was about to hear.

Hanna began to speak. "Tyler, you need to know what has happened to Vena. I know she doesn't want you to know; the simple woman thinks you would leave her if you knew."

Tyler's head rose. "I can't leave her; she has to know I love her more than life."

Hanna took a shaky breath. "Well then, you need to know what happened to her five years ago. It started when we hadn't heard from Vena for a few days, which was odd because we talked every day. She had just told John it was over between them. Of course, he protested, and for a while, he even stalked her. That stopped after she had gotten a restraining order against him. Although he still called, cursing at her and threatening her, but he never came near her." Hanna exhaled before she continued.

"Vena tried to ignore it all and continued her regular routine, teaching her classes. We knew Vena was afraid, but she hid it well and there was always someone around. We called her almost around the clock. Then one day we called as we usually did, but she didn't answer the phone. We then rode to the studio. The studio was locked up, and it just appeared as if no one was at home. After several times calling and going to her house, we went to the police. We explained our fears to the police, but they said there was nothing they could do if she hadn't been missing for at least 72 hours. After a day had passed, we went back to the police, begging them to come and just check it out. They knocked on the door and still didn't get an answer. We were finally able to convince the police to break in the door. We found John lying on the couch, passed out in a drugged haze. The house was wrecked. We searched downstairs and still couldn't find Vena anywhere. After a minute, we heard Dee screaming from upstairs. She found Vena in the bathroom, unconscious, naked on the floor, and handcuffed to the pipes." Hanna paused, handing him the photos. "These were the injuries Vena suffered." Tyler stared at the pictures and cursed. Her eyes were swollen shut. Her hair had been cut off almost to her scalp and dried blood was on her face from a broken nose. She had bruises on the neck, chest, arms, and legs, where he had beaten her. Tyler looked up at Hanna with rage so deep, it surged through his body. If he saw John at that moment, it was no doubt in his mind he wouldn't hesitate to kill him. Tyler dropped the pictures to the floor. His shoulders slumped forward, and heavy tears fell from his eyes to the floor as he silently wept. Dee, Mary, and Hanna held on to each other, watching with tears also flowing down their faces.

Tyler gathered his composure, stood and said in a decisive, but shaky voice. "I'll stay with Vena," he informed them. "I'll call when I've come up with the best way to protect her." He turned to go upstairs, then stopped and faced the girls. "Thank you for being in her life," he said to them and then continued upstairs.

Tyler sat beside Vena's bed as she slept. His gaze lovingly searched her face. He would give his fortune for just one day with that dirty bastard. Various emotions went through Tyler like a flood. Rage was the dominant emotion, but there was also the guilt he felt for not being with her when she needed him the most. He fell to his knees beside the bed and prayed for strength to control the rage that wanted to explode within him. He prayed for Vena and the life they were destined to share. He thanked God for allowing him back into her life. Tyler then dropped his head beside her and cried as he had never cried before.

When he could cry no more, he rested his head on the bed and fell asleep.

Vena woke feeling dehydrated and groggy. She felt Tyler's head near her hand. Gently, she caressed her hand over his head. She loved him so much and did not want to lose him because of her past. John Matthews may have destroyed her, but she would not allow him to destroy the love she knew she and Tyler could have.

His head rose. "Hey, Classy."

He rose to sit on the side of the bed, pulled her into his arms, and cradled her head against his chest. Still under the influence of the medication, Vena gave him a weak smile.

"You okay?" Tyler asked.

"Thirsty," was all she could get out.

"I'll get you something to drink; be right back."

When Tyler went downstairs, he took the opportunity to call the girls and asked them to meet at Vena's loft. He decided it would be better if they all kept an eye on her.

He returned with a glass of water. Vena trembled slightly, so he helped her to drink.

"Tyler, can you hold me," she slurred. She laid her head on his chest and closed her eyes.

"Did they tell you about John?" she asked softly. "I'll understand if you don't want…" she began.

Tyler put a finger under her chin, tilting her head up to face him.

"Open your eyes, Classy," Tyler demanded gently. "I love you. I'm not going anywhere. Got it?"

Vena nodded, relaxed in his arms, and immediately fell asleep. He laid her down and went to meet her friend's downstairs.

****

"Hey, how is she?" Hanna asked when everyone had arrived.

"Better," Tyler answered. "I am not going to allow her to run away. Hanna, I want you to call this company." Tyler handed her a card. "They are the best security company in the state." He then faced Dee and Mary. "Get all the numbers you think John would try to contact Vena. Give them to Hanna. They will provide a trace on all incoming calls to her. Cedric, Tom, and Robert, I need to make a trip to the south side of Chicago. We need to find John Matthews, if only to keep one step ahead of him. You game?" Tyler asked the men. "Between us all, we will be able to discreetly keep an eye on her. The only thing we cannot do is allow Vena to know what we are doing. Okay?"

"We got your back, man," Cedric offered.

Although the girls looked worried, they agreed.

"Don't worry, ladies. As bad as I want to get him, I won't jeopardize my friends for that piece of shit." Everyone went into action.

Vena woke, still disoriented from the medicine. She searched the room and found Tyler asleep on the chaise lounge. He looked so uncomfortable with his long legs dangling over the edge of the lounger. Vena slid from the bed. She stood still a second to allow the dizziness to pass.

"Hey, you," Tyler said, getting to her before she fell. He helped her sit on the side of the bed.

"Why are you sleeping on the chaise?" she croaked from her dry throat.

"I didn't want to disturb you," he told her. "How do you feel?" he asked with concern in his eyes.

"Okay, but hungry," she stated.

"Can you walk downstairs?"

"Of course," she said, although she still felt a little woozy. Together they prepared omelets. They sat and ate, neither speaking. Finally, Tyler broke the silence.

"Classy, why didn't you tell me about John?" he asked.

"I was ashamed and I didn't want to relive that time, but it looks as if I'm going to relive it anyway," she stated. Vena dropped her head. "You always said he was no good. I should have left him back then. I just felt so sorry for him. See what my kind heart got me."

"I'm here now, and I won't let anything or anyone hurt you again," he promised.

"I know you won't, Tyler." She looked at him with confidence.

"I've installed an alarm system. You will have to know how to set it. Okay?"

Vena lowered her head again. "Tyler, I can still hear his threats," she admitted.

"Don't worry; it's going to be alright now."

"I want to ask you something," Vena said. "Now that you know the horrible things he did to me; do you still feel the same?"

He took her hand. "Look at me," he demanded. Her head rose slowly.

"I love you, Classy; never doubt that. I'll never leave you. Come on, let's go to bed."

****

Three months later

Already three months were behind them. Time had moved on so quickly after her scare.   Now she could focus on the dance company's success and the première of Vena Thorn's Dance Troupe. John hadn't tried to contact her. Maybe prison gave him time to think and he's moved on with his life, at least she hoped he did. Vena gradually dropped her guard. Tyler was not so at ease. He ensured that if he wasn't with Vena, someone was watching her. Vena didn't seem to notice.

Vena wrapped herself into the Dance Company and school, and together with the troupe, they had created a fantastic repertoire. The dancers and staff worked hard, giving their all in the preparations for their premiere performance. It was scheduled for January in Chicago's Omni Theater, where the company will debut.

Hanna managed publicity, and already advertising and promotions were decided and soon to be presented to the public. Mary took care of all the financial matters, and Madame Thurston handled all monetary donations. Dee, along with the dancers, worked on costuming and stage design, leaving the final decisions to Vena. Since the news of her dance company went public, her studio enrollment doubled. Everything seemed to fall into place, and she was pleased; so much so, Vena became more relaxed and happy. Ever since John's release, Tyler had stayed with her every night, and she was happy. She started sleeping more, and her increased appetite put a smile on Tyler's face.

Their first repertoire will feature the music of Stevie Wonder. Vena watched as the dancers rehearsed a dance she choreographed to *"Ribbon in the Sky."*

"Good, I like that, but Guy," she instructed, "pirouette and then lift Stacy." They nodded and repeated the step. "Perfect. How does it feel?"

"Good," they both said.

The phone rang. "I'll get it," Vena called to the girls in the office.

"Vena Thorn's Dance Company, can I help you?" Vena said into the receiver.

"Can I talk to Vena?" the deep voice asked.

"This is she. Who's calling, please?" she asked.

You know who this is, bitch! You didn't think I forgot you, did you? When you least expect it, I'll be there, and I'll get you. You hear me, bitch?!"

Vena dropped the phone and fell to her knees. Stacy and Guy rushed over to Vena, calling for the girls.

Hanna ran into the studio, followed close by Dee and Mary. "What's wrong?" they shouted frantically.

They explained someone was on the phone. Hanna quickly picked up the phone; she could hear John still shouting and cursing. Vena was on her knees, breathing heavily and clutching her chest. Mary pushed her way to Vena.

"Is she okay?" Guy asked, concerned.

"Take a break upstairs while we deal with this, please," Mary calmly instructed.

"You rotten bastard!" Hanna screamed into the phone. John hung up.

"Vee, breathe; come on, honey," Mary said, kneeling beside her on the floor.

"My chest hurts!" she moaned, clutching her chest.

"Call 911!" Mary yelled.

Vena lay on the floor; her heart was racing and her breathing was impaired while Mary tried to keep her calm.

The ambulance arrived minutes after the call, and the EMT's quickly began to work on Vena.

"Relax, Miss; we are here to help you," the paramedic said as they administered oxygen and checked her vitals. "We are going to transport you to the hospital."

"I'll ride with her," Mary informed Dee and Hanna and followed the gurney. "Someone call Tyler!" Mary shouted.

They arrived at the Glendale Hospital in record time. An ER doctor attended to her immediately.

"I can't catch my breath!" Vena panted. The doctor took her blood pressure, encouraging her to relax.

Hanna rushed into the room with Dee behind her. "What's wrong with her?" Hanna asked, concern etched on her face.

"Her blood pressure is dangerously high. We must bring it down. Is she on pressure medicine?" the doctor asked.

"No. She had a severe upset. Is she going to be alright?"

"Whatever frightened her has brought it to this level. Don't worry; we'll get it back to normal. I need to get some blood work and an EKG just to be sure it wasn't a heart attack."

A nurse came in, prepped her for an EKG monitor, and took blood. Another nurse arrived and gave her medication to regulate her pressure.

"Now you relax so your pressure will go down. I'll be back after your tests are in," the doctor told her, patting her hand.

After the doctor left, Hanna took her hand. "It's going to be okay, Vee."

"Hanna, will he ever stop? I can't live with the constant fear that John will one day find me. How can I bring Tyler into my dysfunctional life?"

"Vee, Tyler loves you."

"I know, but is it fair to him, Hanna? I mean, come on."

"Vee, you are supposed to be calm," Hanna said, rubbing her hand.

Vena sighed, "Okay, I'll try." She paused. "Hanna, I'm scared," Vena declared.

"I know. It's going to be okay. Tyler will see to that."

Vena had just closed her eyes when Tyler rushed into the exam room.

"Tyler," she said, relieved to see him.

"Baby, you alright?"

"No!" Hanna interrupted. "John called the company threatening her, her blood pressure shot up, and she had chest pains, so we rushed her here. Tyler, try to keep her calm, so it won't rise. The doctor said they're waiting for the results of her blood test."

"Tyler," Vena said, "I'm sorry."

He kissed her forehead.

"Don't worry. I'll take care of John," he assured her.

"Tyler, please don't do anything that…"

"Sh..." Tyler and Hanna said. "What's keeping the doctor," Tyler said anxiously.

"I'll go see," Hanna offered.

Vena looked up at Tyler. He was angry but held his anger in check; she knew it was for her sake.

"How did he get my number, Tyler?" Vena asked.

"I'm sorry. I forgot about the dance company ads," he answered.

"Will he ever leave me alone?" Vena asked, frustrated. "I don't want to live the rest of my life looking over my shoulder."

"We got him now. He'll be back in prison tonight," Tyler informed her.

"How?" she questioned, anxiously hoping what he said was true.

"I had your incoming phone calls traced by the phone company. They'll have him on tape making terroristic threats to you."

"Are you sure?" she asked, afraid to believe it.

"He's on probation; any contact with you will put him back in prison to finish his term.

Vena closed her eyes and exhaled. "Is it really over, Ty?" she asked, hopeful.

"Yes, baby, it's really over."

Hanna, Dee, and Mary came back to the room. Tyler kissed Vena, excusing himself to confirm what he had told her.

"You okay?" they asked.

"I am now. John is going back to prison for a long time," Vena informed them.

"Thank God," Hanna said, relieved. "What did the doctor say?" she asked.

"I don't know. He hasn't come back yet."

The doctor entered a few minutes later. "Vena," the doctor said, frowning. "When was your last period?"

"Period? I haven't had a period in about three months. I'm going through menopause. Aren't I supposed to stop now? I am 50," she told the doctor.

"Normally yes, but you're pregnant."

"No, I'm not," Vena said firmly.

"Your blood tests indicate you're pregnant. How pregnant, you will need to see your OB/GYN," the doctor replied. Vena looked at the man as if he'd sprouted horns.

Hanna, Dee, and Mary, after their initial shock, started grinning. Vena looked over at them.

"Don't you dare laugh; I mean it." The girls were thrilled.

"Don't you dare be happy, damn it. My son is twenty-nine years old, and I'm too old to have children!" Vena cried, distressed.

"No, actually," the doctor interjected, "you have a young body for a fifty-year-old woman."

"She's a dancer," Dee announced proudly.

"Well, there you go," the doctor added, smiling. "Congratulations," he finished and left the room.

"This is great, Vee," Dee said.

"Why is it?" she pouted.

"You and Tyler are going to have your own baby," Dee said excitedly.

"On no," Vena interrupted. "You can't say anything to Tyler!"

"Why?" Hanna asked, confused.

"Ty doesn't want children," Vena stated.

"How do you know that?" Mary frowned.

"He's fifty-two years old. He has no children anywhere," Vena supplied.

"That doesn't mean he never wanted any," Hanna affirmed.

"Come on, Hanna. What other logical reason is there, huh?"

"I think you should tell him anyway, Vena. It's his child too," Dee said logically.

"Tell him what? Oh, by the way, old man, we are going to have a baby," she said mockingly.

Hanna and Mary laughed.

"Hey Vena," Dee asked, "You're not thinking...?"

"Never. I could never do that," Vena replied with sincerity.

"This is great," Hanna clapped her hands gleefully. "We will have a little one around."

"So when will you tell him?" Mary asked.

"I don't know. I have to feel him out first, but I'll tell him. Whatever happens, happens."

When Tyler returned, the girls were giggling and then suddenly stopped when they saw him enter the room. He frowned, looking at each one suspiciously. "The police will pick John Matthews up today."

Tyler looked at the monitor above Vena's head. "Great, your pressure is down. Now we can go home," Tyler said happily.

Later that night in the bed, Vena's head rested on Tyler's chest.

Vena asked, "Why didn't you ever have children, Tyler?"

"Didn't want any at the time," he shrugged. "I wouldn't have been able to share in their life. I was too busy building my business. I just didn't have time. Then, I didn't even have time for a wife."

"Did you love your wife, Ty?" Vena asked curiously

"No. After I had time to think about it, I believe I married her because I was lonely, and everyone else I knew was married. So, I tried it for three years; I'm surprised she stayed with me that long."

"Did it hurt you when she left?"

Turning his head, Tyler looked at her frowning. "Why so many questions?"

"Just wondering." Vena paused. "Ty, didn't you ever want children?" she continued.

"Vena?" He frown as he leaned up on his elbows to look at her.

"Did you?"

"Yes, I did at one time, but I'm happy without them." He lay back down.

Vena became quiet. She moved away from him, pulled her nightgown over her head, and dropped it to the floor. She then rolled on top of Tyler and outlined his lips with her tongue. He caught it and pulled it into his mouth. He wanted her too.

"Are you sure, Classy?" he asked huskily against her lips.

She responded by kissing him deeply. He pulled away again. His hand roamed down her body, feeling the curve of her sexy behind.

"Tell me you want me," he demanded huskily

She tried to kiss him; he rolled her on her back.

"Tell me," he insisted. He let his hand slide between their bodies, and he began to caress her softly, gently probing.

Vena sighed and closed her eyes.

"I want you inside me, Tyler," she whispered.

He captured her lips as he slowly entered her. Their lovemaking had always been a battle of wills, each wanting to control their pleasure and neither gaining the ability.

Tyler started noticing a difference in Vena. He just couldn't figure out what that difference was. He knew she was busy with the company's first performance, but it wasn't that. Mary, Dee, and Hanna were unusually quiet, which was curious.

He did notice Vena ate more than usual and seemed to be tired more times than not. She never knew he had seen her, but he recalled last week after midnight she was in the kitchen eating ice cream, a jar of olives, and drinking soda.

She was hiding something; what, he didn't know. Every night, she wore her nightgown to bed, and if they made love, she would remove it beneath the covers.

Something was going on, and he meant to find out what. He had talked to the boys; they agreed with him, that the girls were unusually quiet. He had cornered Mary, Dee, and Hanna; they all claimed they had no idea what he was talking about.

Tyler arrived home earlier than he expected. Vena was in the shower and having a singing good time. He smiled when she sang off key, thinking he would just slip in the shower with her. She was standing sideways when he entered. What he saw knocked him for a loop. Vena was pregnant. Her usually tight stomach was swollen and well rounded.

"Vena!" Tyler yelled.

She jumped and turned to face him, apparently surprised. She groaned. Tyler was angry - no scratch that - he was livid. How could she deceive him by not telling him she was carrying his child? Tyler turned to walk out.

Vena ran, out of the bathroom still wet from the shower.

"Tyler, wait!" she called.

He stopped and turned to her. Hurt with a mixture of anger was on his face.

"Why, Vena?" he asked.

"Let me explain, Ty."

"What's to explain, Vena. You could have told me you were pregnant. Why the big secret?"

"Let's talk about this, Ty. I'll be…"

"No, not now; I'll see you later." He stormed out of the room. Vena stood there naked with her mouth dropped open, shocked at Tyler's reaction.

Vena stared dumbfounded at the door Tyler had just exited. Realistically, he had every right to be upset, and she was willing to give him the space he needed. "*He'll be back. He'll be back,*" she told herself.

Vena dried herself, slipped on a T-shirt and a pair of sweat pants then went downstairs to get something to eat. While rummaging through the fridge, she remembered Tyler saying he was happy without children. What if he doesn't want this baby?

"Oh God," she groaned. She wanted this baby. At four months pregnant, she knew she should have told him before she started to show. However, she didn't expect to show so early in the pregnancy. Well, he knows now, so she will have to wait to see how he feels when he returns.

*****

The doorbell rang. Expecting it to be Ty and thinking he had left his key, Vena pulled open the door. Before she could shut it, John had grabbed her by the throat and lifted her off the floor. He pushed her into the room and kicked the door shut.

"Did you really think I was going back to prison before I got you, you bitch? This time, I will kill you," he spat venomously.

Vena clawed at the hand around her throat, gasping for air. All she could think about was the child she carried. Just when she thought she would lose consciousness, he dropped her in a heap to the floor. Vena coughed and again gasped for air. She tried to crawl away from him; too late, he grabbed her hair and pulled her to her feet. He grabbed for her neck again.

"Please, John, don't do this," she pleaded.

John sneered at her. "Do you think I forgot you put me in prison?"

Vena screamed.

"Shut up!" he shouted, then punched her in the face.

Vena felt her nose crack as blood trickled over her lips. She fell over the coffee table and landed on her knees. She tried to crawl away, but he halted her escape by stepping on her back and pinning her to the floor. All Vena knew was she had to protect the baby she carried at all cost. Vena turned to her back and kicked with all her might between his legs. John doubled over and fell to his knees. Vena took the opportunity to run upstairs. Mentally, she cried out for Tyler. She was almost to the top when he grabbed her ankle and pulled her down the steps like a rag doll.

"No, you don't!" he spat at her. "You owe me five years of my life, you slut, and I'm going to take it from your ass. Did you think I was going to let you get away with sending me to jail! When they find your body, I'll probably go back inside but not before I poke you in every hole you have!"

Vena lay sprawled on her back, slightly dazed. Through blurred eyes, she saw him fall to his knees. She tried to push away from him, but he grabbed her leg. He began to unbuckle his pants. Vena panicked. She attempted to scream but nothing came out. She used her free leg and kicked as hard as she could into John's chest. He fell back and lay stunned for a moment. Vena rose quickly and started to run. Despite her dizziness and blurred vision, she got away.

John gave chase while still holding his chest. He tripped her, causing her to fall with a thud to the floor.

"Oh, now you want to fight back. I should have killed your black ass five years ago. I told you, you won't ever get rid of me."

John was enraged. His breathing was heavy, sweat ran down his face, and determination gleamed in his eyes that caused fear to grow in her. John had been a handsome man at one time, but years of alcoholism and drugs had taken a toll on him.

He grabbed her arm and pulled her up, only to hit her in the face. The punch was so hard, her head snapped back. When he pulled back to hit her again, she dug her nails into his face; when he grabbed her wrist, she bit his hand until she tasted blood. If she were going to die, she would die fighting, she decided.

He cursed and punched her twice in the head until she released her teeth from his hand.

Vena stumbled and fell to her back. Barely conscious, she started kicking wildly. He caught her leg, his fingers biting painfully into her ankle as he fumbled with opening his pants. Realizing his intention, Vena fought as if her life depended on it. He meant to rape her. Not again, her mind screamed. Don't let him rape you again, she prayed. She clawed at the hand that pinned her leg. As long as her arms were free, she knew she had to fight, and Vena fought fiercely with all her might.

Panting and briefly stunned, John straddled her and began pummeling her face. Blindly, she swung at him and fought against the darkness that threatened to take her. It almost rendered her unconscious. She tasted blood in her mouth and felt the swelling of her face from each blow he inflicted on her until blissful darkness took her.

****

Tyler drove around for a while, finally ending up at Hanna's house. He knew she would tell him why Vena kept this from him. He was infuriated with her. How could she keep her pregnancy a secret from him? Damn it, he loved her. Why couldn't she trust me?

Tyler rang the doorbell. The door opened. By Tyler's expression, Hanna knew something was wrong.

"Hey Tyler, is everything okay?" she asked concerned.

"Can I come in?" he asked.

"Sure," Hanna said, moving aside and closing the door behind them.

"Did you know?" Tyler asked bluntly.

"Yes, I knew," she told him. Hanna didn't have to ask what he was referring to.

"Why didn't she tell me?" Tyler said through clenched teeth.

"She didn't think you wanted children," Hanna simply stated.

It then dawned on him; that's why she had questioned him that night.

"Why didn't she talk to me about this?" he said angrily.

"Come on, Tyler. Who has children at fifty," Hanna replied. "She's afraid you would be upset. Where is Vee…?"

"Hey," Robert called from the den, "you have to see this."

Hanna went to see what he referred to. Tyler followed.

"Look at this. Hey Tyler," Robert greeted.

Repeat, John Matthews eluded police after his arrest for terroristic threats to the dancer Vena Thorn. Matthews was released from prison four months ago after serving time for the attempted murder of said dancer. An All-Points Bulletin is out on John Matthews.

Any information, contact Crime Hotline at your local police station.

Tyler didn't hesitate. Right away Tyler knew just where John Matthews was. "Call the Northbrook Police, Hanna. Send them to Vena's. Robert, let's go," he ordered.

"I'll follow you," Hanna told them.

"No," Tyler said, "there might be ..."

"I don't care," Hanna interrupted. "If he has hurt Vena, I'm going to be there; so I don't care what you say, I'll be right behind you."

Robert and Tyler sped off to Vena's house. The car came to a screeching stop in the driveway. The car had barely stopped when Tyler jumped out and raced up the stairs to the loft. He eased open the door and witnessed John straddled over Vena, beating her.

"Yeah, bitch, you're mine now!" John yelled at her. A low, fierce growl came from Tyler as he ran crashing into John, knocking him off Vena. The two men slid across the wood floors. Before John could react, Tyler began pummeling him with his mighty fists. The police arrived minutes after Hanna. Robert tried to pull Tyler off John, but Tyler had the strength of ten men. The three officers and Robert could barely pull him off Matthews. Hanna ran up the stairs, where she found Vena lying on the floor.

"Oh, my God!" she screamed. "Vena!" Hanna fell to her knees beside her.

"Call 911 right now! Oh Vena, please Vena, open your eyes," she cried. "Please open your eyes, Baby."

Tyler broke free from Robert, ran to Vena, and fell to his knees. He was stunned at the damage John had inflicted on her.

"Check her pulse," he cried. "Classy, wake up. You can't leave me now, you can't."

Hanna pressed her fingers to her neck, "Yes, yes a faint pulse."

The police managed to restrain John, pulled him to his feet and take him to the door; he looked over his shoulder at Vena on the floor.

"I hope the bitch dies," he spat. Robert punched him so hard in the face, he knocked him out cold.

Tyler and Robert exchanged a look of respect, and at that moment, an alliance formed between them.

"Vena, please open your eyes, baby, open your eyes," Tyler coaxed. "God, please help me, help her," Tyler prayed as tears streamed down his face.

Her face was a pool of blood. One eye was swollen shut, her lips were swollen and cut, and bruises were on her neck where John had tried to strangle her.

Vena moaned and moved her head. She could barely see anything; all she could see was shadows. Vena began to fight, her arms swinging wildly.

"Vena, Vena, it's me, Hanna!" she cried.

Hanna had a hard time restraining her. Tyler reached over and easily restrained her.

"Vena, it's okay. We're here," Tyler reaffirmed. "Vena, I'm here, I'm here, baby."

Vena turned her head to his voice. She reached up to touch his face. He took her bruised hand and brought it to his lips.

"I love you," she mouthed through swollen, split lips before darkness consumed her again.

"I love you too," he replied. The tears that filled his eyes rolled slowly down his cheeks.

The ambulance arrived, and the paramedics moved them aside to administer care to Vena.

"What happened?" the attendant asked.

"She's been beaten. Is she going to be alright?" Tyler asked with concern.

"Her pulse is weakening; we have to get her to the hospital now."

"I'll ride with her," Tyler called as he followed the paramedics.

"Robert and I will follow. I'll have to call Dee and Mary," Hanna called after him.

The police had taken John into custody, and the ambulance was in route to the hospital.

"Vena, I'm so sorry baby," Tyler whispered, rubbing her hand in his.

Minutes later, the ambulance came to a halt. The attendants rushed Vena into the ER. Tyler followed close behind, but a nurse stopped him.

"Sir, you can't go there. We'll…"

Tyler looked down at the nurse with unbridled rage. "Lady, if you don't move, I swear…"

"Tyler!" Hanna called, rushing to him. "Tyler, don't," she said, stopping him from doing something drastic. She apologized to the nurse as she pulled Tyler away.

"Come on, Tyler," Hanna said, leading him to the waiting area.

"Hanna, I can't live my life without her. This is all my fault. If I hadn't..."

"No, it's not, Tyler. You didn't know he would get away, so don't blame yourself for this. She's going to be okay. We have to believe that."

Tyler knew that, but the rage in him was consuming his mere existence.

It had seemed like hours before the doctor beckoned them. Tyler and Hanna joined him in Vena's area. She just regained consciousness. She has a concussion; how severe, I don't know yet, but she will survive."

"What about the baby?" Tyler asked.

I'm not pregnant. Who are you people; where am I? What has happened to me? Vena thought, confused as panic started to rise.

She tried to rise and scream when the pain coursed through her body. She fell back on the pillow.

"My head, help me, please help me!" she pleaded.

Tyler looked over at the doctor. "Help her; she's in pain, Doctor. Please do something."

"I'll give her a mild painkiller until we find out the condition of the baby she carries. She's been through a beating no woman should have survived, but she did, thank God. We must see if the baby she carries is okay," the doctor informed them.

Hanna stood by, watching and praying for her friend.

"Okay, doctor, just help her, please."

Tyler looked at Vena. He could see she was suffering, and it pulled at his heart.

The doctor instructed the nurse to administer a pain reliever into the IV tube.

Beating? What are they talking about? Vena thought

The nurse returned and injected the drug. Vena sighed when the pain subsided in her head. Her eyes slowly shut.

The doctor lifted the bloody shirt, exposing her rounded belly.

He looked at Tyler. "You're sure she's just four months?" he asked.

"Yes, I'm sure. Is there a problem, doctor?" he looked worried.

"No. No, she's just a little large for four months, that's all."

"Let me see," the doctor said when the technician arrived with the ultrasound equipment. He placed gel onto the paddle then placed it on her belly.

A picture started to form. Hanna and Tyler's eyes were trained on the screen.

"Oh, I see," the doctor said. "There are two healthy babies in there, with strong heartbeats I might add."

"Twins!" Hanna and Tyler echoed.

Her eyes opened groggily.

"Can you see our babies, Classy? We have twins."

"No, I'm not pregnant," she mumbled as her eyes closed.

"Let her rest," the doctor instructed. "She has been through a lot, but the babies seem to be fine; strong heartbeats," he again reassured Tyler.

"Let's get her bandaged up and comfortable, so she can rest. I would like to keep her a few days. I see no other injuries, but I want to see if she sustained any head injuries. I'll send for you when we have completed her test."

"Thank you, doctor," Tyler said. "You're sure she will be alright?"

"So far, other than superficial bruising, she is fine."

"Thank you, doctor," Tyler said, shaking his hand. Tyler and Hanna went to the waiting room to talk to Dee and Mary. They rose when they saw them.

"How is she?" they asked.

"She's going to be okay," Tyler sighed, relieved.

Hanna, Dee, and Mary hugged each other.

"How's the baby?" Mary asked.

"Their heartbeats are strong. I saw my babies," Tyler announced proudly.

Dee frowned. "Babies?" she repeated perplexed.

"Yes, Vena's having twins," he announced.

The girls hugged happily.

"Oh, Tyler, this is great. What did Vena say?" Mary asked.

Tyler frowned. "Something's not quite right. She keeps saying she's not pregnant and was in a lot of pain, so the doctor gave her something. She is resting now. When she wakes, she'll get everything together, I'm sure," Tyler said confidently.

"Oh yes, it's just the excitement of everything."

"Great news," Hanna announced. "The news just reported John is back behind bars."

Tyler exhaled a sigh of relief. Killing John wouldn't have been enough for what he'd done to Vena. If Robert and the police hadn't pulled him off John, he was sure he would have done the chore gladly. He knew he could have. Now Vena can relax and enjoy the rest of her life without fear from that bastard.

The girls and Tyler waited for word from the ER doctor on Vena's tests.

A few minutes later, the doctor came to them.

"She has a severe concussion; I want to keep a close eye on her tonight. We have her on medication that should help. Don't worry, the medicine shouldn't affect the babies; they will be fine."

Tyler and the girls sighed relieved.

"Can we see her?" Dee asked.

"If you're very quiet. We want her to rest so she can heal," the doctored commented sternly.

"We will," Mary promised.

The four of them gently opened the door to Vena's room.

Although she was now cleaned up, the extent of her injuries was more visible. Her face was bruised and swollen, tape stretched tightly across the bridge of her nose, and her lips were swollen and cut.

"She looks a lot better than she did a few hours ago," Hanna said quietly.

Vena opened dazed eyes. Her head didn't hurt anymore. She stared at the people around her bed and wondered who they were.

The girls moved closer to the bed.

"Hey Vee," Hanna said softly.

Vena looked at her through blurred eyes.

"Who are you?" she slurred out, then her eyes closed.

Hanna looked at Tyler. Tyler shrugged his shoulders.

"It's probably the medication," Mary said. "We should come back tomorrow."

"Yes, I think you're right," Dee said.

"We'll see you tomorrow, Tyler," each one said and kissed his cheek. "She's going to be okay."

Tyler nodded, yet he looked worried.

"Don't worry, Tyler. I'm sure it's the medication. We'll see you, later," Hanna said.

When the girls left, Tyler pulled up a chair and sat beside the bed. Vena turned her head at the sound. Her eyes opened.

"Hey, Classy," Tyler said softly.

"What is your name?" she slurred. Her eyes blinked slowly and opened. "Are you my prince charming? What is your name?" she repeated.

"It's me, Tyler," he answered.

She frowned. "Are you here to save me, Tyler?" she asked.

"Always, Vena," he responded.

"Who is this Vena I keep hearing about?"

"You are Vena," Tyler answered, looking at her oddly.

"No, no my name is--my name is ..." she slurred and her eyes closed.

This bothered Tyler. Maybe it's not the medication, he thought. Maybe she genuinely doesn't know. Tyler needed to get in touch with Hanna. He remembered her saying Vena had a therapist; maybe it's time to call her.

Tyler was emotionally and mentally tired, but he was not about to leave her here alone. He thought he would just rest his eyes for a minute.

Chapter Six

Vena awoke a little dazed, but awake. Her head still throbbed, although not quite as severe. She looked around the room. There sleeping in a chair was the man with the large, strong, gentle hands she saw earlier. She tried to clear her throat, but it was a little sore. He didn't budge. She tried again a little louder. Still no response. After reaching for the box of tissues on the bedside table, Vena threw them at him and hit him square on the head. Startled, Tyler sat up quickly and went to her bedside.

"Hey, Baby, you're awake."

"Who are you?" she asked sharply.

"You don't know me?" he countered.

"Should I know you?"

"Yes, of course, you do. I'm Tyler Kinson."

"Why don't I recognize you then?" she asked warily.

"I don't know, Vena," Tyler replied. "You really don't know me, do you?"

"No."

"What do you know?" Tyler asked, trying not to sound alarmed.

She was silent for a minute. "I can't remember." She paused. "I remember this hospital," she said quietly. "Should I remember more?" she asked. "Wait. I remember someone said I was pregnant. They must have made a mistake. I cannot be pregnant." Vena frowned. "Am I married?" she asked him.

"No."

"There you go. That is why I'm not pregnant," she stated, terribly sure of herself.

"Feel your stomach," Tyler instructed.

Vena's hand ran down her belly. "What does that mean? I'm just fat," she retorted.

Tyler smiled. "Trust me, Vena. You are pregnant."

"And how would a complete stranger know this?"

"Because I'm the father."

Vena shook her head. "You and me? I don't believe..." Her tone panicked, "Who are you?"

"I think maybe I should call your doctor," he replied, turning to go to the door.

"What happened to me?" she called after him.

"You can't remember what happened, or how you came to be here, Vena?"

"My name is not this Vena," she replied harshly.

"Then what is your name?" he asked her.

She was concentrating. "Um... wait, I know my name," she said, pausing.

After my minute she said, "I don't know my name. What's going on, Tyler? This is scaring me. I can't even remember what I was doing last month. Oh God, what's going on? Please, can you help me remember?" she asked eagerly. Visibly shaken, her eyes filled with tears.

He took her hand. "Don't worry, Vena. I'll take care of you, okay?" Tyler said gently, calming her.

She nodded, holding on to his hand and not wanting to let it go.

"Vena, let me call Hanna. I'll be right back."

"Tyler," she paused, "You promise?"

"Yes, Baby, I promise," he reassured her.

She let his hand go and watched as he went through the door.

Tyler left the room, pulling out his phone to call Hanna.

"Hello..."

"Hanna?"

"What is it, Tyler?"

"It's Vena. I think she's lost her memory," Tyler reported, troubled.

"What do you mean, she lost her memory?" Hanna asked frantically.

"She remembers nothing, Hanna. Could you call her therapist and tell her about Vena?"

"Okay, I'll call right now. We will be at the hospital as soon as possible. Maybe she will remember us."

"I hope so, Hanna, I hope so."

When Tyler returned to the room, the doctor was there.

"Good morning, Tyler. She seems better," he said while checking her eyes.

"Do you still have a headache?" the doctor asked Vena.

"Yes, the more I try to remember, the more it hurts. What happened to me, doctor?" she asked.

"You were…" the doctor began to tell her.

"Assaulted," Tyler interrupted.

"Assaulted?" she repeated, alarmed. "Where did it happen?"

"Downtown," Tyler lied.

Vena nodded but frowned. "Downtown, where?"

"Northbrook," Tyler supplied.

"Northbrook? I don't know this Northbrook."

"Vena, what do you remember?" the doctor asked.

Vena became alarmed.

"What's going on?" Vena yelled. "I don't know you people. I don't know you," she pointed at Tyler. "Oh God," she moaned. "I can't think, let me think!" she said, holding her head.

"Calm down, Vena. We'll get to the bottom of this, I assure you," the doctor told her.

"Be calm, doctor? I have no memory. I can't be calm!" she said exasperatedly.

"Trust me, Vena, it will all work out," the doctor reassured her patting her hand.

She calmed a little.

"I'm going to continue to give you a pain medication," the doctor replied, "then we'll retest you to see if things have cleared up. I'll be back to see you later."

Dr. Wood left. Vena looked over at Tyler as tears rolled down her face.

"It's okay. We will figure everything out," Tyler promised.

"I have to trust you. I know no one else," she said, shaking her head.

Hanna, Dee, and Mary arrived. They eased open the door.

"Hi, Vena," Hanna greeted.

"Hello," she returned hesitantly.

"I'm Hanna," she introduced. "This is Dee and Mary," indicating the other two girls with her.

"Vena," Hanna asked, "Do you know who I am? "

"I'm sorry, no; should I?" Vena inquired.

"Yes, we are your best friends," Hanna stated.

"My head hurts. I can't think, I can't think!"

"Vena, I called your therapist," Hanna informed her.

"I have a therapist?" she asked.

"Dr. Hopkins will be here shortly."

Vena was rubbing her temples; her head was throbbing.

Tyler asked, "Is your head hurting?" Vena nodded. "I'll call the nurse."

All she knew was she needed to remember, and this Tyler seemed to know a lot about her. What other choice did she have? These people were the only ones who knew her.

****

A couple of days later, Vena was able to get out of bed. She sat beside the hospital window, looking out at nothing. Nothing seemed familiar. She wondered what city she was in and how she came here. Was this her home or was she from another town?

"Where am I from?" she asked aloud.

"You are originally from Chicago, Illinois, but you reside in Northbrook for about eight years now." Tyler said from across the room.

In a chair sat a mature woman who introduced herself as Dr. Ellen Hopkins, her therapist.

Why are all these people here, she thought to herself? Tyler was with her day and night, always at her bedside. When she awakes, he is there; when she sleeps, he is there. After a few minutes of silence, Tyler excused himself so she could talk privately with Dr. Hopkins. Vena continued to stare out of the window, starting to feel confined to the room.

When those people would visit, they'd talk excessively about nothing she knew about. Tyler would sit in a chair quietly, sometimes looking at her or reading, but he was there. Vena allowed her eyes to look around the white sterile room. She had to get out of here. She couldn't find out who she is if she were stuck in this place with people she didn't know.

Dr. Hopkins remained silent. She didn't try to force her to speak or persuade her in any way.

"What kind of therapist are you?" Vena asked harshly. "Aren't you supposed to make me talk or something?"

"Only when you're ready to talk. No one can make another talk if they have nothing to say, right?" Dr. Hopkins asked. She had been in this hospital four days. Her head still throbbed, it seems, every time she was awake. The doctor said it was because of the severe concussion she acquired from the attack, and there was always treatment for the pain. Then she'd go back to sleep. Right now, all she wanted was to get out of here.

"What happened to me?" she asked the doctor.

"You were attacked."

"Was he captured?"

"Yes," Doctor Hopkins said. "He's behind bars now."

"Who are these people to me that visit so much?"

"They are your friends, Vena."

"I don't remember them. I want to remember; I really do, but it's so hard. Then on top of that, I discover I'm pregnant, and I don't even know the father of my children," she sighed. "I guess this is the case for the crazy people's journal."

Dr. Hopkins chuckled, "Yes, it would be a case for the books. You have amnesia; it's not uncommon when someone has gone through some sort of trauma. The three women that visit are truly your best friends. Let yourself know them; they love you very much, Vena. Now Tyler, he's the father of your babies, and the man you love with all your heart. When you arrived all beaten and bleeding, he never left your side. You held on to his hand that day as if your life depended on it. If he tried to leave, you held on tighter. He was the lifeline that you needed. He hasn't left your side since. Talk to them, Vena. They could tell you a lot about yourself and your life. They love you so much. Just talk to them?" the doctor advised.

Vena nodded. "I will, doctor. I do remember holding on to a man's hand. I felt safe, and I thought if I let go, I would fall," she admitted.

Dr. Hopkins nodded. "Subconsciously, you felt secure with him. I like to think that was because of the love you share. You can trust Tyler."

The session ended. "Call me if you need me, Vena."

Vena agreed. After the doctor left, she was alone. Tyler hadn't returned yet. This was her chance. She looked in the closet, found clothes hanging, and quickly got dressed. She knew she had to get away from this place. With her heart pounding in her ears and the dull ache that began to grow in her head, Vena eased from the room and stepped into the hallway. She had to get her memory back, and lying around in a hospital room wasn't it. Once she was out, she would find something that was familiar to her - anything that would stimulate her memory.

The automatic glass doors opened and she stepped through them, all she knew was she was free. Not knowing where to go, she started up the sidewalk. If she got tired, she would return to the hospital. She looked at everything: buildings, stores, anything that could spark a memory. She had been walking for a while. After a few blocks, nothing seemed familiar. Vena stopped and looked at her surroundings, nothing. She turned to look back. She couldn't see the hospital anymore.

"How far did I walk?" she asked herself. The pain in her head began to throb. She didn't want to admit that she was lost but she was. Now afraid, she started to panic. It was getting dark, and she was cold. She looked up the street again to find nothing familiar. The few people passing began to look at her strangely. She was afraid to ask for directions, let alone talk to more strangers. Walking back into the direction she thought she had come from, she looked for the hospital and realized too late, that she had made a mistake by leaving. She stopped in the middle of the sidewalk, turning this way and that, with burning tears rolling down her face. She was lost, cold, and scared.

Tyler frowned. His heart skipped a beat when he entered Vena's room to find it empty. He was gone a little longer than he expected, but there had been a problem at the restaurant he had to fix. Tyler took a deep breath and relaxed. She probably went for more tests, he decided. Tyler sat waiting, occasionally looking at his Rolex. Thirty minutes had passed. *Did tests take that long?* he thought. He went to the nurse's station.

"Excuse me," he said to the nurse at the desk, "Is Vena having tests done?" he asked.

She lifted a chart and looked at it. "Not today, Mr. Kinson," the nurse confirmed.

"Then, where is she?" he inquired.

"She should be in her room."

"No, she's not there," Tyler said impatiently.

The nurse frowned. "Not there?" she repeated, coming from behind the desk. "Mr. Kinson, the last time I went to check on her, I thought she was in the bathroom."

"She's not there!" he responded harshly. Tyler knew it was not the nurse's fault. Vena wasn't a prisoner. The nurse started to panic. Calmer now, Tyler reassured her.

"I'll find her," he said and left the floor. Tyler searched, thinking maybe Vena just needed to get out of the room for a while. She wasn't to be found. Right away, Tyler knew she had left the hospital.

Tyler called Hanna, Mary, and Dee to get their help in locating her. They each drove around the streets surrounding the hospital. She couldn't go too far from the hospital; she didn't know the city. Tyler's phone rang.

"Hanna," Tyler said over the two-way mobile.

"Where could she have gone, and why, Tyler?" Hanna asked.

"She was tense today. She didn't talk; she just paced the room most of the time.

"Where did she think she was going?"

"I guess anywhere out of that room," Tyler answered.

"She scared. Let's not forget she doesn't know… wait, I think I see her on Elm and Broad Streets." Tyler pulled over to the curb. She was sitting on a bench at the bus stop, her arms wrapped around her body. He got out of the car and raced towards her.

"Vena!" he called.

She turned, and he could see she had been crying. She jumped up and ran straight into his arms. Cold and trembling, she locked her arms tightly around his neck. Tyler lifted her in his arms, and she curled against him.

"I'm sorry. I didn't … God my head hurts. I'm sorry," she kept babbling.

Dee, Hanna, and Mary pulled up behind Tyler and ran from their cars.

"Is she okay?" they asked.

Vena's face was pressed into the crook of Tyler's neck.

"She has pain in her head, but I think she's okay," Tyler answered.

"Oh, Sweetie," Dee said. "It's okay, we understand. We were just so worried about you."

"You scared us, Honey. We care about you," Hanna told her.

"I know you do," she said softly.

She groaned. "Tyler, my head hurts so badly." She held him tighter. He put her in the car, buckling her in as her head fell back with her eyes tightly closed.

"Tyler, I didn't mean to make you worry. I was scared. You don't understand… oh my head," she moaned, grabbing it.

"We'll be back to the hospital soon, Baby. I won't say anything to you until your head feels better," he said, anger in his tone. At the same time, he was relieved.

Tyler carried her in the hospital and to her room. The nurse followed him, and Dee, Hanna, and Mary brought up the rear. Tyler sat her on the bed and began to remove her shoes. He hadn't spoken since he found her. Hanna sent the nurse to get medicine for Vena.

Vena sat there quietly, letting Tyler undress her. Dee handed him a nightgown, and he slipped it over her head. She was cold and in pain, and all she wanted was to lie down.

Tyler was angry; there was no doubt about that. The tenseness of his jaw indicated that. Now was not the time to talk to him. He was working hard at maintaining his composure. He laid her back on the bed and adjusted her pillows.

Vena kept her eyes lowered, too embarrassed to look at any of them. The nurse returned with the dose and administered it to her. She looked up at him and placed her cold hand to his cheek. She gazed straight into his eyes with tears shimmering in hers.

"I'm sorry, Ty," she whispered softly, and then she did something Tyler never expected. She gently pulled his head down and kissed his lips. Lingering a little longer, her tongue inched out to taste his, and he took it in his mouth, loving the taste of her again. When she pulled away, she whispered, "Thank you."

Her eyes shut, and she was asleep.

"Don't think that kiss is going to save you, Miss. I'm still very angry," Tyler announced.

The girls chuckled.

"Yeah right, Tyler. That kiss sure made you madder," Hanna stated.

Tyler looked over at Hanna and the girls, the earlier strain he had felt eased. Tyler smiled.

"She loves you, Tyler, even with the amnesia," Dee declared. "And she called you Ty."

"That's a good sign, right Tyler?" Mary asked.

"I think so," Tyler replied.

"Why did she leave here?" Hanna inquired.

"She's scared," Tyler replied. "I think she'll come around now. Dr. Hopkins says she needs more familiarity."

"It's time we start exposing her to the things she knows. When is she getting out?" Hanna asked. "We need a plan to bring her back to us."

All agreed and together they discussed a plan of action.

Vena awoke the next morning, slightly disoriented. She turned to see Tyler asleep in the chair he had occupied since she had been admitted to this hospital. She wondered if he ever went home. She noticed the dark circles under his eyes, and that he had to be uncomfortable in that chair. Vena rose from the bed and quietly slipped into the bathroom. She returned to the room feeling remarkably refreshed, and somewhat oddly anticipating the events of the day.

"Good morning, Classy," Tyler said.

He rose, yawned, and excused himself. Vena was sitting on the side of the bed when he returned. Tyler sat down in the chair, and put on his shoes. Vena watched him carefully.

"That chair can't be too comfortable," she stated. "Why don't you go home at night?"

"I'll go home when you go home," he stated quickly.

Vena rose from the bed to stand in front of him and look at him.

"I feel bad that I'm the reason you're so uncomfortable," she replied.

"Who said I was uncomfortable?" he asked smiling.

Vena reached out lightly touching the dark circles that formed under his eyes. "The circles under your eyes say you're not getting enough rest," she said as she examined his handsome face.

"Thanks for caring, Classy, but I'm fine."

"Well, do you have a job; I mean, you're here every day?"

"Yes, I have a job. I have people taking care of things while I'm here with you," he said smiling.

Vena began to squirm. She turned from him. Tyler caught her hand, turning her back to face him.

"What is it, Classy? You want to ask me something?"

"Are you still angry with me?" she asked softly.

"Is that why you kissed me?" Tyler countered.

"Are you?"

"You scared me," he stated firmly.

"Are you, Ty? Are you still angry? I know it was stupid. I felt scared, confined, and confused? I'm sorry. I didn't mean to scare you. I just thought I could find myself out there, that's all," she admitted and lowered her head.

Tyler listened to her explain, a slight smile touched his lips.

With his finger, he lifted her chin and looked into her hazel eyes. "Why did you kiss me?" he asked again.

"Ty, are you still angry at me for…"

"No. Why did you kiss me?" he repeated. Vena visibly relaxed.

"Answer, please," Tyler said.

"I don't know," she shrugged. "It felt right at that moment, that's all."

Vena turned away from Tyler, then turned back frowning.

"Was I not supposed to?" she asked.

Tyler smiled a wry smile that made him look sexier than he already did.

Vena felt a desire that was strangely familiar to her.

"You can kiss me anytime you want to," he said, smiling broadly.

Vena smiled back. Goodness, he's good looking. Feeling playful, she pushed Tyler back into the chair and stepped between his legs. She bent forward and placed her lips on his. Tyler pulled her onto his lap, leaned her back in his arms, and intensified the kiss. Vena was taken by surprise, but she didn't resist him. Tyler's tongue slipped into her mouth. she sighed and her arms moved around his neck, her fingers gently caressing the back of his head. Tyler felt her finger on the nape of his neck. She was doing things out of habit. Tyler pulled away and looked at her. Her eyes were closed; absently her tongue traced her lips.

"Mm…" she murmured, "You taste good." Her eyes flew open, and she got up quickly. Tyler was grinning. *She's coming back*, he thought.

"I said that out loud, didn't I?" she asked him shyly.

Tyler grinned down at her. Vena rolled her eyes at him and went into the bathroom, closing the door hard.

I'm hungry, Tyler," she said through the bathroom door.

Tyler was laughing when he called for her breakfast.

Dr. Wood entered a few moments later to examine Vena, who was sitting on the side of the bed. "I understand you had a little excitement last night," he said smiling.

Vena dropped her head with embarrassment.

"Yes, Doctor" Tyler replied. "Someone decided to take a tour of our fair city and got lost." Vena glared at him.

"Let's not take any more trips until you are released, Miss," he scolded, "which I think will be in a couple of days."

"Really," she said, "I can go home... Home," she repeated, frowning.

"Okay, let's get on with this," the doctor said. He examined her, and checked her still slightly red eyes.

"Everything looks good, Vena. The swelling has gone down considerably, and the bruising will fade. How are those headaches?"

"I still get them but not quite as awful as before."

"Throbbing?" he asked.

"Sometimes."

"We'll do another scan and see what's going on. Okay, lay back; let me check the little ones."

Vena lay back, and Dr. Wood placed the stethoscope on her belly.

Hmm... Sounds good. Okay, Miss, everything looks fantastic," he surmised. "Get plenty of rest while you're here, and we'll see you tomorrow."

Tyler stood patiently silent. He was happy about her recovery and taking her home. He needed to tell her some things before she was released.

Both were quiet, each in their own thoughts. Vena sat cross-legged on the bed, her small hand absently rubbing her belly.

Tyler watched her. She was thinking; he could tell by her expression.

"Tyler," she said with her head down, "Are we in love?"

Tyler smiled, "Yes."

"How long have we known each other?"

"Ten or more years."

"Do I love you?"

He thought for a moment, "Yes, I believe you do." Absently, she still rubbed her belly, head still lowered.

"Tell me who I am," she asked. She looked at him.

He began to tell her about her life. Vena listened intently. He left out some things. Now was not the time to tell her. When she was released, they'd talk.

She lowered her head again. "Tell me about the ladies that visit all the time. I like them."

"They are your best friends. You girls have been through a lot together."

She looked at Tyler and frowned. "What happened to me that caused me to lose my memory, Tyler? I mean, my life sounds so great, and I have great friends, and I have you. What happened to me?"

Tyler didn't want to answer that question yet, so he avoided it.

"Did I tell you about your children?" he asked.

"I have children?" she repeated, astonished.

"Yes, Byron and Cheryl. They're grownups now and live on the east coast."

They'll be here by the time you're out of here. Byron, the eldest, is a physical scientist, and Cheryl is a social worker. You're extremely proud of them, and you have an extraordinarily close relationship.

"Do they know I'm here in the hospital?"

"Of course, Classy, we are a very close family."

"So, you are their father?"

"No, you were a widow when we met, but I've been in their lives since they were preteens. I love them very much."

Vena closed her eyes and lay back. She could see flashes of a man, and her head began to pound. She frowned and squeezed her eyes shut. She rose from the bed and went to the window, her hand still caressing her stomach. She had her back to him.

"What is it, Classy?" Tyler asked.

Without looking at him, she said, "What did you call me?"

"Classy."

"Why?"

"I've called you that for years."

"Well, stop it!" she said harshly. "I'm far from being classy. I hate this. I hate this room, and I hate I can't remember anything. What happened to me?" she choked out. She sniffed and wiped angrily at her eyes and pressed her fingers to her head.

Tyler stood behind her, placing his hands on her shoulders.

Vena pulled away from him, moving across the room. "Don't touch me. I don't even know you. Who are you, and why am I here? Tyler, I can't do this anymore. There's someone in my head. I don't know who it is. I think I am going crazy." She lowered her head and wept.

Tyler frowned. He was stunned and a little hurt by her outburst.

Alarmed, Tyler went to her. "Baby, please don't do this. I'm here for you." He pulled her into his arms but she pulled away and stared at him. Tears streaming down her face.

"Vena," he said, "Please don't ..."

She fell into him, her arms tight around his neck. She was crying so hard her body shook. Tyler held her. His heart ached for her and the turmoil she was going through.

As her tears subsided, Vena realized she did feel secure in his arms. She held on to him tightly, her head resting on his chest.

"Tyler, I'm sorry," she sniffed and said in a low voice. "I didn't mean what I said, I'm..." she didn't want to leave his arms.

"Come on, Vena, let's get you in the bed," he instructed. He led her to the bed. She lay down and closed her eyes.

"Tyler, who is this in my head? Every time I close my eyes… he scares me, Tyler. Who is this?"

Tyler took her hand and felt a slight trembling.

"Does your head hurt? Shall I call the nurse?" he asked her.

"No, I'm trying not to take that medicine. I don't want to harm the babies."

Tyler looked at her with pride. If he ever questioned his love for her, her statement made him love her all that more.

"It's mild, Vena. Dr. Wood wouldn't give you anything to harm them. Come on, baby; take it if you need it."

"Okay, call the nurse," she agreed softly. Minutes later, Vena was fast asleep.

Tyler stayed while she slept. He recalled her saying some man was in her head. She was starting to remember, but she remembered John. Tyler's jaw clenched; he rubbed his hand down his face. He was tired. There was no way he could stop her memory of John and the violence he put her through, but he could delay that dreadful time until she was strong enough to handle it. It was too early for her to remember that. Once he got her at home, she would be busy with the company and other activities.

Vena awoke to a darkened room. She felt a fear rise in her chest.

"Tyler," she called out softly.

"I'm here, baby."

"Where?" she asked.

He came to the side of her bed.

"What time is it?" she inquired.

"It's late; go back to sleep."

"Lay down with me, Tyler," she said and slid over.

He didn't hesitate. He pulled her into his arms, her head on his chest. She sighed and went back to sleep.

Chapter Seven

The automatic doors of the hospital opened, and the nursed pushed the wheelchair to a waiting car. Vena was happy about her release from the hospital, although a little tentative about her future. However, if she didn't regain her memory, she would just have to create new ones. Being with Tyler would be an excellent start. Even though she had no recollection of their relationship, he treated her with love and compassion. All the people that were involved in her life were very kind.

Vena envied the Vena she didn't know. Who is this woman that this man loved so much?

When they cleared the doors, Vena felt the sun on her face and experienced an elation she didn't think she possessed. She smiled when she saw Tyler park the black Mercedes near the curb by the hospital entrance. She watched as Tyler sauntered towards her. He was genuinely happy. The stress and fatigue she had noticed on his face had disappeared. There was no doubt about it; Tyler was a handsome man. Can I get an amen on *tall, dark and well proportioned,* she thought? Vena felt a stirring in her stomach, and she knew it was not the twins moving.

He stopped in front of her. "You ready to go home?" he asked.

"Yes," she replied.

Tyler helped her from the chair. Vena thanked the nurse and took Tyler's hand. He opened the door and helped her inside; she sat and swung her legs in. When he joined her in the car, he reached for her hand and brought it to his lips. Vena looked over at him, and the frequent butterflies she experienced came again from his touch.

"Do we live far?" she asked when he released her hand.

"Not too far; are you excited?" he asked.

"I don't know if excited is the right word; maybe anxious, nervous, and even a little scared." She took a shaky breath. "I don't know what to expect, and I wonder if being in your home will trigger any memories."

"Don't worry, Vena. Everything is going to be alright now. We'll be home soon," he told her.

Tyler noticed her looking out the window with keen interest. He surmised she was trying to remember.

In a short while, they pulled into the parking lot of a complex of condominiums, unusually large condominiums. Tyler parked and shut off the car, then turned to face her.

"Vena, there are a few people here. Hanna, Dee, and Mary invited people that know you. We are hoping it will help you to remember something. Are you okay with this?" he asked after his brief explanation.

"It's okay, Tyler. I'm willing to try anything to get my memory back right now. I'd just like you to know, Ty, I appreciate you and your kindness, for staying by my side through all this…"

"I love you, Vena," Tyler interrupted.

"What if my memory never comes back? What if I …"

His lips touched her hand. "Then we will make new memories; we have the babies to look forward to, and just being happy."

She smiled. She knew he was right, and she liked being with him. He gave her a sense of security that she needed now in her darkness.

"You ready?" he asked, and she nodded.

The door opened, and Hanna was the first she saw. Hanna happily embraced her.

"Welcome home, Vee," she said cheerfully.

Mary and Dee hugged her next. Tyler stood at her side. "A few people, Tyler," she whispered. He grinned.

Hanna led her into a large room where a few of the guests stood scattered about talking and mingling. When she entered the room, they applauded her. She was beginning to feel extremely anxious. Reaching out, she took Tyler's hand. He smiled down at her and gave her hand a reassuring squeeze. "These are friends of yours, Classy," Tyler explained. "They were very concerned about you and wanted to welcome you home. Most of them are the parents of your students. Are you okay with them being here?"

She smiled and nodded. As her eyes looked around the room, she saw two young people across the room that seemed familiar to her. First, there was a remarkably handsome young man, the tone of light coffee, with hazel eyes like her own. Beside him was a lovely young woman with thick shoulder length hair, who was about as tall as she was and petite. Her small mouth turned up with a beautiful smile as they made their way towards her.

"Hi, Mommy," the young woman said.

She looked over at Tyler, and he smiled. "You're my children," she said as tears filled her eyes. They both hugged her tightly.

"I'm sorry I don't remember you, but I will," she whispered to them.

"We know, Mom," the young man said. "I'm Byron, and this is Cheryl."

They pulled up chairs and sat with her, talking to her about their lives growing up. Vena listened and even asked questions. They asked about the babies and were glad she and Tyler were together now. She lost her nervousness around the people and was now able to talk and laugh with them, even though she didn't remember.

Tyler was immensely proud of her as he watched her circulate the room. Hanna, Dee, and Mary stood beside him and observed how Vena reacted to those with whom she spoke. Tyler's eyes never lost sight of her. At that moment, Vena's head lifted, and her eyes met his. They gazed at each other openly. The girls smiled, watching the exchange. Vena loves Tyler; she just doesn't remember she does. Anyone could see by the way the two looked at one another they were deeply in love.

The party was starting to break up, and Vena was tired. Tyler could see dark circles forming under her eyes. She hugged Byron and Cheryl and made them promise to visit soon; she promised to call when her memory returned.

After all the guest had left, Vena sat quietly beside Tyler and listened to the girls as they bantered back and forth. She was a little tired, but it had been a lovely day. Seeing her children and meeting people from her life made her feel special. It was a pleasant feeling, she realized, as her eyes closed.

The girls and Tyler went about cleaning. "Let her sleep while we clean up," Mary advised.

Vena dreamt she was sitting with Dee, Hanna, and Mary at a table when Tyler entered and walked to her. The memory was so clear. She could hear music and remembered she was happy to see him. When he reached her, it wasn't Tyler, and the hate she saw in the stranger's eyes was undeniable. A throb started in her temples. Any other time, she would push the memories away. This time, she refused to let it go. She needed to know who the man was that always evaded her memory. The unidentified man was angry and started screaming at her, but she could not hear him. The pain in her head worsened. No, she told herself, don't let it go. The angry man grabbed her. Vena came to her feet. In her mind, he caught her and dragged her across the floor. She was screaming, but no sound came out. The pain in her head was becoming unbearable. Then the vision was gone, but the pain in her head remained. Tears filled her eyes from the severity of the pain; she grabbed her head and fell to her knees.

In the distance, she heard her name being called frantically. She tried to focus on the soothing sound that she had become so accustomed to, which was trying to invade her mind. She wanted to turn her head, but the pain would not let her. Vena felt herself being lifted.

"Mary, get her medicine from the suitcase, please," Tyler asked calmly.

Mary rushed from the room to get the pills.

Vena began to focus and saw Tyler's image. "My head!" she moaned.

"I know, Baby," Tyler said.

Mary returned with a glass of water and the medication. Vena took it with no protesting. Her eyes fluttered and shut, but she was not asleep. When the pain subsided somewhat, she opened her eyes. She looked over at Tyler. He seemed angry. Weakly, she raised her hand and gently cupped his cheek.

"I'm sorry, Ty, to be so much trouble for you." Tyler clasped her hand and brought it to his lips.

"Why are you angry?" she asked, concern in her eyes.

Her eyes were blinking slowly; the medication started to take effect.

"No, Baby, I'm not angry at you," he told her.

She looked at the girls. "I remember something."

"No, Vee," Hanna said, "we'll talk later."

"No, please listen, before I forget," she slurred out.

"Did we meet Tyler at a restaurant one night?" she asked urgently.

"Yes, yes, we did," Hanna confirmed.

"What else, Baby?" Tyler asked. She grabbed onto Tyler's arm. Her nails were digging in but she didn't notice, and Tyler ignored it.

"Tyler, you were coming to see me and when you got close, it wasn't you; it was that man that always comes when I try to remember. Why does that happen, and who is he? He wants to hurt me. Who is he?" she asked frantically.

She pulled at Tyler's arm. Her eyes were closed, and she was fighting hard to keep them open.

"Rest, Vena," Tyler said, trying to soothe her.

"No, I have… to tell you. He grabbed me," she was talking slower, "and he was dragging me on the floor, then... I woke up."

"Okay, honey," Mary said. "You rest; we'll talk tomorrow."

Vena nodded let sleep take her.

"I'll put her to bed. See you tomorrow," Tyler told them.

Tyler lifted her then carried her to the bedroom. He removed her clothes and put her under the covers. He sat for a while, watching as she slept. He loved her so much, and he hated seeing her go through the turmoil in her head. He was glad she was remembering, but he didn't want her to have to deal with the bad things. Softly he kissed her forehead, pulling the blankets up. He was tired and needed to sleep. He left the room and went to his own bedroom. He wanted Vena in his bed, but until her memory returned, he would have to sleep alone.

Vena awoke, disoriented, in the darkened room. Tyler was gone, and she felt the emptiness right away. She had gotten used to him being there when she woke up. She wondered where he could be. She rose from the bed, clad only in her underwear. Barefoot, she exited the darkened room and walked down the hall, noticing the room with a faint light shining out of the open doorway. She looked into the large bedroom where she saw the silhouette of Tyler lying in a large bed. Quietly, she moved to stand beside the bed. She knew Tyler was exhausted; he had never left her side when she was in the hospital. She had a desire to touch him, as if her touch would remove all his fatigue. He lay on his back with one arm thrown over his head and the blanket turned down to his flat washboard abs, exposing his beautifully sculptured broad chest. Vena felt the stirring of desire as she watched him. She wanted him; she wanted him every time she saw him. Was this how she always felt when they were together?

Vena stood in her underwear, her hand resting lightly on her growing middle. She moved over to the other side of the bed and gently lifted the covers so not to wake him. She slid into the large bed beside him. She leaned up on her elbow and studied his face, wanting desperately to touch him. *Tyler is an exceptionally handsome man,* she thought, and he loves me. Did she love him, she wondered? Right now, all she knew was she wanted him. Her eyes lingered on his chiseled lips as if hypnotized. She reached out and lightly traced his lips with her finger. She moved closer to him. The heat from his body radiated under the blanket. Her tongue peeked out to moisten her lips; she wanted to kiss him badly. She moved closer so her body pressed to his. Finally, she leaned over and gently kissed his lips. He jumped, and Vena jerked back. They stared at each other for a moment.

Tyler reached out and threaded his fingers through her hair, pulling her head down; his lips touched hers and eased her mouth open as his tongue slipped inside her mouth. Vena sighed as the kiss deepened. Vena needed to feel his body closer to her; she shifted and rolled on top of him, not breaking contact with his tantalizing mouth. Tyler was nude, and his body heat warmed her. Her hands involuntarily wandered down his body. She needed him inside her. Her mouth left his and pressed soft kisses on his chest and neck, moaning when she felt the throbbing of his manhood against her inner thigh. She wanted him inside her badly.

It surprised Tyler to find Vena in his bed. Her lips on his were his undoing at that moment; it's no way he could stop himself now. He wanted her with a passion; he needed to be inside her. Her touch was driving him to be unreasonable. The warmth of her half-naked body lying prone on him was driving him mad, and he was getting harder with her every touch and every kiss.

He had to have her beneath him. Tyler flipped her onto her back. Surprised, she looked up at his face close to hers. She could feel his hot breath on her face; his breathing was as escalated as her own.

"What do you want, Classy?" he asked huskily. Her tongue traced his lips.

"Tell me!" he demanded gently.

She reached up to kiss him; he turned his head. The hands that were on his shoulders caressed his body as they moved softly down. She felt his pulsating manhood against her, blocked by her underwear. She moved against him. The feeling she received from the movement caused her breath to hitch.

"When was the last time we made love?" she whispered.

"It's been a while," he answered.

Tyler's hands moved down her body and easily removed her underwear; Vena undid her bra and threw it aside. He rubbed against her tauntingly.

Vena moaned and closed her eyes.

"You want me," Tyler stated. This was not a question.

"Yes" she breathed out, "Yes."

"You sure you want me, Baby?"

"Yes," she lifted her head and kissed him. Tyler shifted and entered her. Her moan was audible. Her legs circled his body.

"Tyler," she moaned, "You feel so good."

Tyler stroked her, moving in and out as passion built with each stroke.

He pulled out just to the head of his manhood and slowly slid back into her hot, wet body. Vena lifted her hips to him, and her orgasm pulled him further inside her. Her legs wrapped and tightened around his body. She greedily wanted all of him. Her hips lifted to meet his every move, pulling his essential nature from him and causing him to lose control. He could feel her orgasms, one after the other. He leaned up on his hands and moved, pushing them closer to ecstasy. He was unable to fight the inevitable. Tyler closed his eyes and succumbed to the ecstasy of their lovemaking, and lifted her higher. Vena held on to him as if her life depended on her orgasm. She felt like she was being pulled upward and Tyler was her lifeline. When he came, she grabbed onto him and held on until they both came down from the clouds and were back to reality, both falling asleep in each other's embrace.

Chapter Eight

Tyler still lay sleeping when Vena left the bed to prepare breakfast, dressed in one of Tyler's shirts that hung to her knees. The doorbell rang. Vena opened the door to Hanna, Dee, and Mary.

"Good morning," Vena greeted. "Come in, I'm making breakfast." The girls looked at one another.; Vena was barefoot and wearing Tyler's shirt. Stunned, they followed her to the kitchen.

"Sit, have some breakfast," she offered while getting some cups for coffee.

Hanna noticed right away how relaxed Vena seemed, chattering away. Dee and Mary looked at Hanna, grinning.

"Where's Tyler?" Hanna asked.

"Oh, he's still asleep. I have such wonderful children," she stated. She jumped from one subject to the other. Vena didn't say this much when she had her memory.

"Vee," Hanna interrupted her, "did you remember anything else?"

Vena paused, thinking. She then smiled.

"I remember the way Ty made me feel last night," she grinned, putting her hand to her mouth. Her hazel eyes shined mischievously.

They all burst out laughing.

fuiop That's what Tyler heard when he entered the kitchen. He hated to leave Vena, but he had to see about the restaurant's grand opening plans. He knew Vena would be all right with the girls. He came in, kissed Vena, and bent and kissed her belly.

"Morning, girls," Tyler said, smiling. "What's funny?"

"Oh, nothing!" they said together.

"Sit, Ty, and eat breakfast," she ordered. "I discovered I could cook," Vena said proudly.

Tyler and the girls laughed. Tyler sat and enjoyed his breakfast. "Vena, I have to go into the office today."

"Office? What is it that you do, Tyler?" Vena asked curiously.

"I own restaurants."

"Oh, is it a good job?"

"Very good," he answered, smiling.

"What are you doing today?" Tyler asked Hanna.

"I thought I'd take her to the studio and to see Dr. Hopkins."

Tyler pulled out his wallet and handed Vena a credit card. "You need maternity clothes. You're getting round," he stated, rubbing her belly. He kissed Vena before leaving.

Vena's visit with Dr. Hopkins was something she dreaded. She wasn't sure if she honestly wanted to remember; she was happy as she was.

"Will I ever remember?" she asked the doctor.

"Subconsciously, Vena," Dr. Hopkins said, "you're protecting yourself from the truth, and you feel you're not strong enough to accept it. You'll know when the time is right. When you feel strong enough to accept the truth, that's when your memory will return."

Vena wasn't sure what that meant, but she thanked Dr. Hopkins and met Hanna and the girls downstairs.

They then drove to the studio and sat outside the Roselee Thorn Dance Studio.

"Who's Roselee Thorn?" Vena asked, looking at the building. She had an uneasy feeling when she looked at the door that led to the upper part of the building. There was something familiar about the top floor.

That's your mother's name," Hanna told her. "You named your dance studio after her. You teach dance to children."

Vena stared at Hanna astonished.

"Can we go inside?" she asked.

They got out of the car. Vena was apprehensive, and her eyes kept straying to the door upstairs.

"It's okay; go in," Mary encouraged.

They walked through two doors into the reception area and office. Through the other opening was a large room with ballet barres on three walls and a large mirror on the other. There were about twenty adorable children sitting on the floor with their little legs stretched out in front of them. When the students saw her, they jumped up and surrounded her. One little girl said, "I miss you, Miss Vena." Vena smiled at the small child.

"Miss Vena, did you swallow a watermelon seed? Your belly is round like a watermelon," another child replied.

Vena chuckled, "No, I have two babies inside," she answered.

"When will they come out?" one little girl asked.

"Not for a while," she answered, smiling.

The instructor called the children over to finish their class.

Vena joined Hanna, Mary, and Dee in the office and sat in a vacant chair.

"You okay?" Dee asked, concerned.

Vena nodded but remained silent. Hanna was explaining to her that next door was the dance company studio, when Vena held up her hand. Mary, Dee, and Hanna watched her closely.

"Was I ever at a big theater?" Vena asked, rising from the sofa.

"Wait a minute. Tyler was there, I saw dancing, and you were there too."

The whole time Vena recited what she remembered, the girls were nodding and grinning.

They hugged and laughed, happy that she was starting to remember.

"Wait," Vena said. "That man didn't come when I remembered this time. Hanna, who is that man that invades my memories? He frightens me, I…."

"Let's go see the company's rehearsal studio," Hanna said, thinking fast and cutting her off.

The large warehouse that was renovated into the rehearsal studio for the dance company was next door to the dance studio.

When they walked in, the dancers enthusiastically greeted her. The dancers gathered around, telling her how rehearsal for the premiere was going.

"I'm sorry," she apologized, "I don't remember too much. I'm sure it will be great. Can I see some of the dances?"

They brought her a seat. "This is called *Ribbon in the Sky*," the dancer stated. "You choreographed this piece and most all of them."

Vena watched intently. *I know this*, she thought.

She rose from the chair and went to the center floor. The girls watched with interest. She was remembering. She executed every step in unison with the other dancers.

"Another one," Vena said, winded. The music started, and she knew every step.

"Vena!" Tyler shouted, witnessing her doing a routine involving a run and leap. Vena stopped, looking at Tyler like a child caught taking a piece of candy.

"Tyler, I remember," she said breathlessly, going to him.

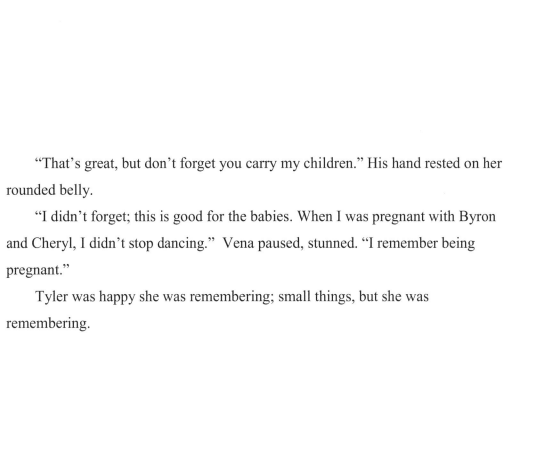

"That's great, but don't forget you carry my children." His hand rested on her rounded belly.

"I didn't forget; this is good for the babies. When I was pregnant with Byron and Cheryl, I didn't stop dancing." Vena paused, stunned. "I remember being pregnant."

Tyler was happy she was remembering; small things, but she was remembering.

Chapter Nine

Tyler lay on his side and watched Vena languidly rub her belly. She quietly stared at the ceiling, seemingly deep in thought. Their twins were starting to get restless and were kicking more frequently. Vena says it felt like the babies were fighting each other for more space. By rubbing her belly, they seemed to calm, and their mother could get to sleep.

Vena softly said, "I love you, Ty." Her eyes closed and she was asleep.

Tyler chuckled and tenderly kissed the side of her head. "I love you too, Classy."

Tyler was awakened by Vena's restlessness in the bed.

"John, please don't do this!" Vena screamed. "Don't do this." Vena was having a nightmare. Tyler shook her gently, calling her name.

"No, John, don't; please stop!" she screamed. Tyler shook her harder.

"Vena, wake up, wake up!" he shouted.

Her eyes opened, glazed and afraid. She backed away from him, fell to the floor and scrambled to the corner of the room, still pleading with her tormentor.

"Please don't hurt me anymore!"

Tyler was on his knees beside her, trying to wake her, but she fought him and pushed him away.

"Vena, baby, it's me Tyler!" he shouted.

"Tyler, help me. Where are you?" she screamed.

"Vena! Vena!" he shook her again. "I'm here, baby, I'm right here!"

"Tyler, where are you? John, please don't. Tyler, where are you? I need you! Tyler, please help me!" she cried.

Tyler continued to shake her. Vena shook her head, slowly becoming aware. Alarmed, she stared at Tyler and then threw herself into his arms, crying uncontrollably.

Tyler held her tightly as she trembled violently in his arms. She held on to him, her heart pounding in her chest. Tyler consoled her, spoke to her softly, and reassured her, wanting her to feel safe.

When her tears subsided, Tyler helped her to the bed. She remained very quiet and deep in thought.

"You okay?" Tyler asked.

She nodded but didn't speak.

"Is your head aching?"

She shook her head.

She jumped slightly and pressed her hand to her stomach.

Vena looked over at him.

"The babies?" he asked.

"I think I woke them up," she said with a half-smile.

She didn't mention the dream, and he didn't ask her about it.

"I'm hungry," she stated.

"Come on, I'll fix something," Tyler told her, helping her to her feet. He pulled on bottoms while Vena put on his shirt.

Vena sat quietly while Tyler made her a western omelet. She watched, but she wasn't focused. Tyler set a plate in front of her and sat across from her at the breakfast bar. He watched her silently as she ate. He hated she had to go through this and felt helpless not knowing how to help her. He wanted her to regain her memory but was it worth this? He would love her even if she never got it back.

"Tyler," she spoke finally. "I've been thinking. Maybe I should go away somewhere, away from you, so you don't have to deal with my psychosis problem.

I mean, I'm such a burden to you and – well - you won't have to worry." Even as the words left her mouth, her heart was breaking. She didn't want to leave him, but was it fair to him to burden him with her problem? "I mean, Tyler, is it fair?"

Tyler stood up so fast he knocked the stool over he was sitting on. He couldn't believe what she was saying.

"Shut up!" He yelled so loud, Vena jumped.

"Damn it, Vena, damn it. What are you saying? You want to leave me? Where will you go, huh? Who's going to be there when you have nightmares? Tell me, Vena!"

Startled and surprised at Tyler's anger, Vena stood up.

"That's the point, Tyler: you won't have to deal with them anymore. Do you think I like not knowing who I am, or the headaches, the nightmares? Do you think I asked for this? I don't even know what happened to me, or why it happened. Damn it, I hate seeing you so tired, watching over me, not sleeping at night because of me. I… "

"Shut up, Vena!" Tyler yelled.

"I will not!" Vena yelled back. "I'm going, Tyler, and you can't stop me!" She turned and walked away from him. He grabbed her arm, turning her to face him.

"Vena, don't test me," he warned.

She pulled her arm away. "I'm tired of being vulnerable to you - to doctors - to myself. I need to go away so that I can get my head straight. Don't you see, Tyler? I'm doing this for you, because I love you. I don't like seeing the pity in your eyes when you look at me. I don't want your pity, Tyler. Do you hear me! I don't want it! I'm leaving!" She walked away from him.

"Vena, you walk out that door, I swear I'll ..."

Vena stopped; her hazel eyes were brown from anger.

"What Tyler!" she yelled at him. "Beat me like John did; chain me up; is that what you'll do!"

Tyler took a step toward her; she backed up as her head started to throb.

"Vena," Tyler said more calmly and took another step toward her.

She backed up again. She put her hand up to stop his approaching her.

She remembered. "I remember," she said softly.

"Vena," he called her name and reached for her.

"No!" she cried and backed away.

"Vena, please… let me," Tyler started saying

"No, no, Tyler, no." She turned and walked out of the kitchen.

Tyler followed her. "Where are you going?" he asked.

"I have to go there. I have to go to my loft. I have to know if… I've got to remember if…"

"Vena, wait!"

"No, Tyler, leave me alone, please. I have to do this now."

Tyler caught her and held her. "Okay, I'll take you."

She pulled away, looking up at him. "Okay."

They drove silently to the loft. Tyler was glad he'd had the loft cleaned. He parked in front. Vena didn't wait for him and got out of the car. She stood at the bottom of the stairs, looking up. She was scared. She couldn't remember if John had raped her again, and she needed to know because she would never have mental peace if she didn't know for sure.

Tyler stood behind her. The babies moved, and her hand went to her belly.

"Vena," Tyler said, "You don't have to do this," he put his arm around her.

"Yes, I do," she said and pushed him away from her before climbing the stairs. Tyler was close behind her.

He unlocked the door and pushed it open. Vena stepped inside and walked through to the living room. Her heart was pounding in her chest. She stopped at the spot where John had been beating her; everything came flooding back to her. Her hand instinctively went to her stomach. She remembered thinking she had to protect her baby.

She turned to Tyler, who stood not far from her. "Did he rape me?" she asked.

"No, he didn't get a chance; I came and pulled him off you."

She covered her face with her hands and wept, relieved.

Tyler was beside her in an instant.

"Vena Baby, please say something." She uncovered her face, which was streaming with tears.

"I wish I didn't remember," she hiccupped and lowered her head.

Tyler took her head in his hands, forcing her to look at him.

"It's a good thing you remembered, so you can move on. You understand everything now; no more headaches and no more nightmares. You can remember the good things now."

She pulled her head from his grasp. "How can you stand to touch me, Tyler? I'm so ashamed."

"No, Vena," Tyler said. "You shouldn't feel ashamed. Vena, I love you; that's all that matters to me. We are going to have a wonderful life together, I promise you with all my heart."

"Why would you want to, Tyler?" Vena asked him malevolently.

Tyler's eyes filled with tears, and he stated, "I can't bear life without you. Even with all we've been through, I've never been happier. I need you, Vena, and you need me; we are one. We have so much to look forward to." His hand rested on her stomach. She looked down at his large hand across her belly, then she looked up at Tyler, and her hand covered his.

"I love you, Ty. I love you so much," she said then walked into his arms.

"Let's go home," Tyler suggested. She nodded and left the loft.

They sat in the car.

"Tyler, get rid of the loft," Vena stated, looking up at her former home.

"Are you sure?" he asked.

"I can't live there anymore."

"Okay, I'll take care of it."

They silently drove home.

Epilogue

Vena stood sideways in the full-length mirror, her pregnancy very apparent. The official grand opening of Tyler's new restaurant was turning out to be a gala affair, and the Who's Who of Chicago would be attending. Vena looked at herself again. The dress was beautiful, white with silver thread throughout it and an emperor waistline to accommodate her growing children. The neck was cut low and rounded, showing a bit of her cleavage; the sleeves were long and cut full on an angle. She pulled her long hair back into a sleek chignon, and her ears were dressed in diamond teardrop earrings Tyler had given her because he wanted to, so he said.

Tyler came up behind her, peering in the mirror at her and grinning.

You're beautiful," he murmured in her ear.

"The dress is," she responded.

"So are you, Classy."

She sucked her teeth. "What's beautiful about this big belly?" she said, rolling her eyes.

"Because you carry my children, our legacy," he placed his hand on her stomach, "and you're even more beautiful carrying our children."

Vena smiled. "You are so charming, and you're right - I am beautiful." The babies kicked, and Tyler laughed, "They agree."

"They've been doing a lot of agreeing lately, Ty."

"You okay?" he asked, concerned. It was close to her time to deliver; he was worried and a little scared.

"I'm all right," she said, patting his hand.

Tyler did as he promised. He rented the loft out so she could still have the studio where it was. It was better that way. Vena moved in with Tyler instead of finding a place of her own.

On occasion, she had nightmares and some headaches, but nothing severe. The babies were healthy, and so was she. The girls were thrilled her memory had returned. Byron and Cheryl   came as soon as Tyler told them their mother was back. Hanna, Dee, Mary, and Vena were their old chatty selves again, and the Vena Thorn Dance Company received rave reviews when they premiered, and the company will be on tour after the babies are born.

Madame has already declared she is the grandmother to the babies and was helpful with the premiere of the company; she took care of arranging the company's touring calendar for the upcoming season.

 However, tonight was Tyler's night for the Grand Opening of the last Den, and it promised to be a grand event. Everyone that was invited confirmed his or her attendance.

Tyler was trying to fix the bowtie to his tuxedo. Vena took the task in-hand.

"Ty, I have something for you," she whispered before lightly kissing him on the lips. Vena handed him an envelope.

"What's this?" he asked, frowning at her.

"What could I give the man who has everything?" she said. "So I thought this was something you would especially love. Go ahead, open it."

Tyler opened the envelope. Inside was a card; the front read:

I love you with all my heart. My gift to you is

Tyler looked up at her, opened the cover, and lifted the picture inside.

A son and daughter

Tyler looked at Vena, his eyes filled with tears. He looked again at the ultrasound picture of his children. He pulled Vena into his arms as the tears streamed down his face.

"Thank you, Classy, for my babies," Tyler sniffed.

Vena pulled away from him and looked at the tears of joy rolling down his cheeks.

Vena's eyes filled. "Tyler, you are going to make me ruin my makeup." She turned and looked in the mirror.

"I'm complete," he said, kissing her on the neck. She turned in his arms, and his lips met hers for a quick kiss, which turned into a passionate kiss.

Tyler broke the kiss.

"Hey, how about if we skip the gala, stay here and go to bed," he said, wiggling his eyebrows.

Vena pulled away. "No, Tyler, we can't, this is a special night for you, and everyone is expecting us."

Tyler nibbled on her neck.

"We can't," she moaned. "Can we? No, no we can't," she said, pulling away from him.

"You made this night special already," he said, pulling her back into his arms. "A quickie," he said, nibbling on her ear.

"Ty, no. We don't have quickies."

Tyler released her. "You're right; we don't," he laughed.

"Come help with my shoes." Vena had stopped seeing her feet about a month ago. She sat on the bed and lifted her foot.

Tyler slipped the satin white heels on her feet. He frowned, "Are you going to wear these?"

Vena looked down at him. "Why wouldn't I? They match my gown."

"Okay, Classy, fine," but Tyler knew he'd better bring her slippers just in case her feet started to swell. The stretch hummer was out front. They had to swing by and pick up Hanna, Dee, Mary and their dates.

They arrived at the restaurant; the place was full to capacity. Tyler entered with the very pregnant Vena on his arm. The area was large, and this restaurant was different from the others. This one incorporated banquet rooms, a VIP section, as well as fine dining. The atmosphere was soft and classic. Waiters walked around and served samples of the cuisine. There was entertainment, a band with a group of male singers, and later in the evening, there would be awards presented and keynote speakers.

After mingling, Vena began to feel tired. She found her table right in front of a large dance floor; also seated at the table were Madame, Hanna, Dee, Mary, and their dates. She didn't see Tyler anywhere, which was odd; he was hardly ever out of her sight. Maybe he was busy with some last minute details.

Vena smiled as everyone chatted happily around her. If anyone had told her she would be this happy, she would never have believed it.

"My dear, you look radiant carrying my grandchildren," Madame said proudly.

Vena smiled, "Madame, I feel radiant tonight because this is Tyler's special night."

Vena had taken off her shoes and kicked them under the table. A waiter stood in front of her with a covered tray.

"Excuse me, Ms. Thorn; Mr. Kinson wanted me to bring you these." He removed the lid from the tray and held out her slippers. Vena took them, thankful Tyler had thought of it. She thanked the waiter. He bowed and left her.

Everyone at the table laughed, except Vena. She gave them all a warning look and rolled her eyes.

"Where's Tyler?" she asked.

Everyone shrugged. Vena frowned at them.

"What's going on?" she asked, knowing something was not quite right.

"Hanna, Dee, Mary, you guys know something," she accused.

"Vena, whatever are you talking about?"

Vena leaned towards Madame. "What's going on, Madame?" she whispered.

"I'm sure I don't know, my dear," she whispered back.

She turned to all at the table, her narrowing eyes glaring at them.

"You know," she said, "you all know, don't think…" then she heard Tyler's baritone voice. She turned to the floor. Her eyes widened. Tyler wore a microphone headset and was saying such lovely words.

Then Vena remembered the song *"The Promise"* by the Temptations, her favorite song.

Tyler stepped down from the platform and stood in the middle of the floor with the other singers harmonizing behind him.

Vena's hand covered her mouth in surprise. Tyler was singing to her. She always thought he had a great singing voice, and now he was singing to her in public. Tears of joy filled her eyes.

When the song was almost over, Tyler took her hand and lead her to the center of the floor; he then pulled her into his arms and danced with her. The audience was on its feet, applauding. He stepped from her, held her hand and sang. Tears streamed down Vena's face; she tried to smile, but her lips trembled instead. Tyler sang with his heart. It was expressed in his singing and on his face. The backup singers harmonized perfectly. When the song ended, Tyler bent down on one knee.

"Classy," he asked, "Will you marry me?" He held up a ring case and opened it to show her the ring. Tears of joy streamed down Vena's face. She managed to choke out a y*es*.

Tyler's head bent with relief. "Did you hear that, little ones?" he said, kissing her rounded belly. Vena threw her head back and laughed. The music started again, and the group of singers started singing. The guests were encouraged to join them on the dance floor. Tyler and Vena were so engrossed with each other, they didn't notice the other couples on the dance floor.

Tyler kissed her tenderly on her lips.

"Classy, my love lost found, I love you."

The End

Dear Readers,

I hope you truly enjoyed Volume 1 from the Found Love Series. The Holland family journey will continue as they seek love, happiness, and success. Stay tuned and watch as they become a formidable force that will keep you on the edge of your seats. I humbly thank you for being my "sidekicks" on this journey. Again, keep on reading and I will keep on writing.

Vivi

Facebook: Vivian Rose Lee
Email: vivianroselee22@gmail.com

CPSIA information can be obtained
at www.ICGtesting.com
Printed in the USA
LVHW081506130120
643457LV00018B/2140/P